discussion paper:

Working Future ?

Jobs and the Environment

This study is the first in a series of research
reports published by Friends of the Earth
as part of its Action Programme for Positive
Change.

FRIENDS *of the*
earth

Friends of the Earth is:

- The largest international network of environmental groups in the world, represented in 52 countries.

- One of the leading environmental pressure groups in the UK.

- A unique network of campaigning local groups, working in 260 communities in England, Wales and Northern Ireland.

- Largely funded by our supporters. Over 80% of our income comes from individual donations, the rest from special fundraising events, grants and trading.

Friends of the Earth Trust is a charity which:

- Commissions detailed research.

- Provides extensive information and educational materials.

Friends of the Earth, 26-28 Underwood Street, London N1 7JQ

Contents

Acknowledgements:

This paper was written for Friends of the Earth by Tim Jenkins and Duncan McLaren of the Sustainable Development Research Unit.
The authors would like to thank the following for their support, comments, advice and guidance:
Jonathan Bray, Dr David Elliot, David Gee, Paul Hackett, Roger Higman, Mike Jacobs, Nic Lampkin, Andrew Lees, James Marsh, Vicky Pollard, Charles Secrett, Romney Shovelton, Liana Stupples, Fiona Weightman and Fiona Weir.
As ever, responsibility for any surviving errors remains with the authors.

Printed on recycled paper
Design: Cristiana Accettola

Working Future ?
Jobs and the Environment

November 1994 © Friends of the Earth
Published by Friends of the Earth Trust Limited
Charity number 281681
ISBN 1 8570 242 6
Friends of the Earth, 26-28 Underwood Street, London N1 7JQ
Tel: 071 490 1555 Fax: 071 490 0881

Introduction: Sustainable Jobs, Sustainable Environments

Amongst the many difficulties confronting this country, two stand out: unemployment and environmental degradation.

Over the past decades, orthodox economic development has raised living standards for the majority. But it has also caused both these deep-rooted problems. Long dole queues and high levels of ecological damage are key indicators of an unsustainable society.

The challenge, as we cautiously creep along the sustainability path, is to marry sound economic performance with environmental priorities, rather than playing one off against the other or choosing between the two.

This report by Friends of the Earth points a way forward. It shows that public policy and private enterprise can create substantial numbers of jobs, and wealth, by looking after, not abusing, nature. Cutting pollution, conserving natural resources and otherwise protecting the environment can also stimulate efficient economic production, reduce costs for firms and householders and improve industrial competitiveness - while putting people back into work.

In that respect, its findings are likely to confound the conventionally wise. Many of those who populate boardrooms, Party hierarchies and media desks across the country, think that 'the environment' is yesterday's luxury, yesterday's issue, yesterday's news.

How wrong they are.

•••

Unemployment has recently leapt to the top of every Party's economic agenda. There are between 2.5 and 3 million unemployed in the UK. In May 1994, Kenneth Clarke as Chancellor summarised the new consensus by declaring that "unemployment must be the main preoccupation of economic policy-makers in the 1990s".

The Government has come a long way since 1991, when Norman Lamont, as the then Chancellor, declared that unemployment was a "price worth paying to secure low inflation".

There is a danger, though, that environmental priorities will be sacrificed to conventional economic nostrums. Perhaps even worse still, conventional measures to stimulate economic activity, in a break with past results, are increasingly unable to deliver social goods like jobs.

Advocating environmental protection and resource conservation cuts little ice with decision-makers in the Treasury, Department of Trade and Industry and the other Ministries who determine what happens in the economy. "Don't you know", they say reprovingly, "conservation costs jobs and money".

Each Party has its own preferred mix of policy, private sector and public expenditure ingredients for the perfect job creation cocktail. But all agree that economic growth - more production and more consumption - is the essential stimulant.

And that's where the trouble begins, because the bitter after-tastes of this heady brew are conveniently ignored - wasted energy, minerals and other materials, polluted drinking water supplies and filthy air, toxic wastes and contaminated land, acid rain and climate change, bulldozed wildlife habitats and a thinning ozone layer.

As an alcoholic dispels a hangover with another drink, so the cure for economic recovery is usually more of the same: growth as a panacea for all ills, environmental as well as social. "Don't you know", go the reproaches of the the conventionally wise, "without economic growth, we can't create the wealth we need to solve environmental problems".

The Orwellian circularity underlying this argument - economic growth is good, OK it degrades the environment, so we need more economic growth to pay for repairs, creating more damage, requiring more growth to cure, and so on ad infinitum - escapes its proponents. An ever-escalating spiral of degradation is unsustainable and cannot be maintained.

For industry, improving commercial competitiveness too often means cutting costs by shedding labour, and working to boost short term profit margins in order to increase dividends to shareholders. Output and worker productivity rise, but the traditional knock-on effect in labour markets does not occur.

The phenomenon of jobless growth has been marked in the United States, Australia, Canada, and in the UK, where recovery from the recent global recession has been underway for some time.

The consequences of putting profits and shareholder returns above other considerations, and a fiscal regime which encourages this behaviour by taxing labour, often translates into redundancies and lay-offs. The electricity utilities are a case in point.

In autumn 1994, for example, Norweb announced that 1,200 jobs would go: even though profits rose by 116% over the preceding four years since privatisation and the company anticipated dividend growth of between 6-8% in real terms every year up to 2000. Over these five years, industry analysts estimate that the twelve regional electricity companies in England and Wales will shed between 20-25% of their existing jobs - another 18,000 people dumped on the dole queue. By 2000, analysts estimate these companies will likely accumulate total net cash reserves of over £2 billion.

Senior managers running such companies think they are doing a good job. By current commercial standards they probably are, but not by the sustainability criteria for the future.

It's as crazy to penalise jobs and work through taxes, as it is to subsidise environmental degradation, pollution and waste by not accounting for their full costs during production.

A sustainable society must aspire to and achieve wider environmental, economic and social goals than these narrow and selfish interests. Sustainability is about realising 'win-win-win' changes, where interrelated environmental, economic and social goals are met simultaneously by public and/or private sector actions.

To achieve them, though, will require a fundamental shift in policy, commercial practice and public values as profound and long-lasting as those which spawned the Industrial Revolution.

•••

Any reasonable description of a sustainable society must prioritise both employment and conservation goals. Sustainability is about meeting essential human as well as natural needs.

Sufficient evidence already exists, in the UK and abroad, to feel confident that a huge, untapped potential to stimulate employment and improve environmental performance exists in five key industrial sectors: pollution control, energy, agriculture, materials use and transport.

But these benefits will not be realised spontaneously by market forces. It is a fact of human nature, and so business behaviour, that only the rare individual and the rare company innovates: most simply continue as they are until persuaded or compelled to change.

Hiding behind the invisible hand of the market has for too long been an excuse for ignoring the responsibility to govern. Government must take the lead and alter the rules governing the market.

The costs of inaction are high. In 1993, the State spent £8 billion supporting the 1 million long-term unemployed. The benefits of going green, on the other hand, are considerable: from improving the environmental quality of life and meeting international conservation obligations; from reducing benefits needs and boosting tax revenues; from helping to resolve the debilitating consequences of unemployment for individuals and communities.

There are three priority areas for government action. First, certain ideological blinkers must be shed. In various ways, Germany, Japan and the United States show that targetted environmental regulation and high environmental quality standards often improve economic performance, stimulate investment in environmental technologies and services, and create more jobs overall. We can see these positive effects in the pollution control, energy efficiency and materials reuse sectors.

Second, tax regimes must be reformed. Taxes should be adjusted away from penalising economic and social 'goods' like jobs (national insurance) and work (income tax), to deterring environmental 'bads' like pollution and wasteful energy and other natural resource use. So-called green taxes are the principal way in which the full costs of environmental degradation can be fairly reflected in the price of resources and consumer goods. Encouraging energy and resource use efficiency is likely to be essential for improving productivity and competitiveness in domestic and export markets.

Third, public expenditure must reinforce sustainability goals. The money Government spends in sectors like agriculture and transport can readily be used to raise employment and environmental standards simultaneously. (It doesn't matter a jot whether this is criticised as subsidy or praised as investment because, while the amounts may vary, this money will always be spent).

Friends of the Earth will be actively using our findings to prompt government, industry and the public to reject the twin fallacies which have prevented environmentally sustainable development.

As one trades union so graphically put it:
"the real choice is not jobs or environment. It's both or neither. What kind of jobs will be possible in a world of depleted resources, poisoned water and foul air, a world where ozone depletion and greenhouse warming make it difficult to survive." [1]

The future is green.

Charles Secrett
Friends of the Earth.

Employment and Sustainable Development

"The most basic of all needs is for a livelihood: that is employment"

Global economic development continues to cause long-term and often irreversible environmental damage as well as failing to provide sufficient jobs. Yet many of the wide and powerful interests ranged in defence of the economic status quo continue to claim that environmental protection costs jobs. This paper provides evidence to indicate that this claim is flawed.

Not only does environmental protection on balance create jobs, but environmentally sustainable development is compatible with full and rewarding employment. In the long run opportunities for adequate employment will only exist if environmentally sustainable development has been achieved. But in the short- and medium-term too, almost all studies of the effects of environmental policies show that they lead to a net gain in jobs [2]. Far from having to make hard choices between environmental destruction and the social damage associated with the misery of long-term unemployment, these twin evils can, and must, be tackled together.

For centuries, global economic development has depended on the ability to deplete natural resources, to draw down the regenerative capacity of living systems, and to discharge pollution to water, air and land. Over the last few decades the development path followed by the richest nations has accelerated the process of environmental degradation to the point where it now poses a threat not only to us but to other nations, to our children and to future generations. In short, we are approaching the environmental carrying capacity of this planet.

"...employment is not directly linked to the measures of economic success used by governments and firms..."

If the worst effects of the ecological crisis are to be averted, economic and environmental policies must be integrated to keep development within environmental constraints. This is encapsulated in the goal of sustainable development which *"meets the needs of the present without compromising the ability of future generations to meet their needs"* [3, p.43]. From this definition it is also clear that employment is central to sustainable development, as acknowledged by the Brundtland Report: *"The most basic of all needs is for a livelihood: that is employment"* [3, p.54].

This is a vital need which conventional economic development is increasingly failing to meet. Governments, as Norman Lamont, a former UK Chancellor of the Exchequer, so cynically put it, have considered cyclical unemployment as a *"price worth paying"* [4] for keeping wages down in an economy. But the International Monetary Fund (IMF) [5] has highlighted that unemployment in developed countries is increasingly linked to long-term structural change. The IMF also warns that such unemployment may establish itself at a higher level than after the last recession [5]. The European Commission has highlighted the problems of high youth and long-term unemployment rates, large disparities in regional unemployment, the proportion of unskilled persons in total unemployment and the shortage of labour for highly skilled occupations [6]. In response, governments of the richest nations: the G7 countries [7], have attended a special 'jobs summit' to address the trend of persistent joblessness [8].

One of the fundamental reasons for this situation is that employment is not directly linked to the measures of economic success used by governments and firms. Increasing profitability - the main measure of success for any firm - does not always increase employment in that company. In fact, reducing employment is often regarded as desirable

Figure 1: GNP and Employment

Rise in GNP and Civilian Employment in the U.S.: 1950-88

Source: Economic Report of the President, 1989. Cited in Renner[55].

in order to increase labour productivity and hence profits. In the past it has been assumed that in a dynamic economy employment will grow as the total volume of goods and services produced has expanded to offset the labour-saving effects of automation in certain firms and sectors. Increasingly, however, this is not the case.

Economic growth, as measured by increases in Gross Domestic Product (GDP), does not bring a directly proportionate rise in employment (See figure 1). To achieve full employment under these circumstances would require unsustainable levels of economic growth, given current rates of resource and energy use and levels of pollution.

There are two ways in which sustainable development is not directly related to economic growth and profitability. Firstly, that these traditional measures of economic success do not directly consider employment.

Secondly, the environmental damage caused by economic activity is not adequately accounted for. In most cases, firms do not pay the full environmental and social costs of their activities and therefore can increase profits at the expense of the environment and wider social needs. Similarly, national indicators of economic performance, such as GDP, actually undervalue the environment by treating activities that erode the soil, contaminate air and water, and diminish forests and fisheries, as contributions to income rather than as consumption of natural capital.

These conventional measures of success need to be reformed to account for environmental priorities such as minimising pollution in all forms, maintaining renewable natural resource flows and conserving habitats. New measures and indicators which reflect such priorities should be adopted by policy makers in order to gauge progress towards environmental sustainability. For example, an Index of Sustainable Economic Welfare (ISEW) has been developed in the United States as an alternative measure of overall economic performance which accounts for social and environmental factors [9]. The Index subtracts *"expenditures necessary to defend ourselves from the unwanted side-effects of production"* [9, p.70], such as the costs of pollution control and road traffic accidents, from the value of production. It also attempts to account for the loss of environmental quality and future long-term

"...society as a whole can seek 'win-win' outcomes, where economic, social and environmental goals are met simultaneously..."

environmental liabilities which do not involve direct expenditure, such as the depletion of non-renewable resources and the loss of wetlands or farmland. Social factors accounted for in the Index include the value of domestic labour such as housework and child-care, and the inequality of income distribution. The ISEW has also been applied to the UK

Figure 2: ISEW and GNP in the UK

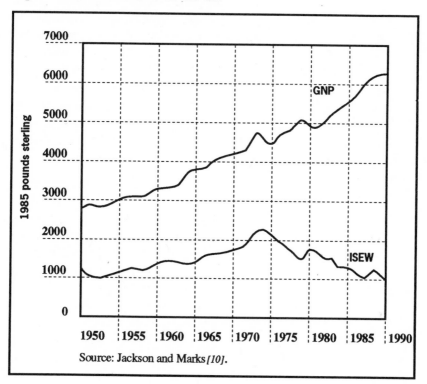

Source: Jackson and Marks [10].

"...Louisiana has experimented with the use of an emissions-to-jobs ratio in policy measures as a method of encouraging sustainable economic development..."

economy [10] and, like the United States, has been shown to follow a substantially different path from GNP (see figure 2). This analysis suggests that real human welfare and well-being, as represented by this Index, has in fact declined in the UK since the early 1970s, rather than continuing to grow in line with GNP.

In the United States the state of Louisiana has experimented with the use of an emissions-to-jobs ratio in policy measures as a method of encouraging sustainable economic development [11]. This simply calculates the ratio between jobs and pollution emissions for a plant, company or sector. In general, the less pollution associated with each job, the more beneficial the activity is, both environmentally and in terms of employment. Targets for reducing the emissions-to-jobs ratio can be used to coordinate economic and environmental policies. Rather than relying solely on environmental policies to reduce emissions and economic policies to create jobs, this approach encourages integration of economic and environmental priorities in policy-making.

On a smaller scale, fully incorporating environmental costs in companies' measures of profitability would also promote sustainable development. Both employment prospects and the natural environment could benefit. If firms have to pay the full costs of energy and resources, and of cleaning up or preventing pollution caused by their activities, then it will become financially more attractive to reduce total production costs by cutting these costs rather than cutting labour costs by shedding jobs. For example, the development and uptake of cleaner technologies which use less energy and raw materials and produce less pollution has been inhibited by barriers such as inappropriate types of regulation, lack of research and development support and limited information [12, 13]. A fundamental

"... it will become financially more attractive to reduce total production costs by cutting these costs rather than cutting labour costs by shedding jobs..."

shift in the balance of costs could help overcome these barriers.

In this way, society as a whole can seek 'win-win' outcomes, where economic, social and environmental goals are met simultaneously [14]. For example, a balanced and well-judged programme of energy conservation can reduce pollution and the threat of climate change; provide householders and industry with lower fuel bills; **and** increase employment. Similarly, developing and installing cleaner technologies in industry not only results in cleaner air and water, but also leads to improved human health and, in the longer term, reduced health care costs and increased industrial efficiency and potential for exports.

Managing the Change

Achieving sustainable development will require far-reaching changes in many economic and social areas including lifestyles and consumption patterns. A comprehensive assessment of the employment effects of the shift toward sustainable development must look at the whole economy rather than individual sectors or firms. Despite the long-term interdependence of environmental protection and employment, the transformation to a sustainable economy will involve job losses in particular industries and particular locations at particular times. Such losses are likely to be more than compensated for by other job gains.

During the transition to a sustainable economy, it is unclear where and when job losses and gains will occur at the same time and where and when the gains will come later. Job gains may not be located in the same geographical area or industrial sector as losses. There may be short-term net unemployment in particular regions. The Government will need

17

to play a leading role in designing and implementing environmental policies that minimize these transitional employment costs *[15]* and establish compensatory programmes where necessary. Several types of countervailing measures have been suggested, including regional policy, retraining schemes and public environmental programmes *[15]*. Overall, Government needs to adopt a strategic approach, establishing targets, and conditions by which those targets can be met by private sector actors to facilitate the change-over and achieve the sustainable development goals of maximising employment prospects while conserving natural resources and protecting land, air and water quality.

In the past conventional economic development has led to significant unemployment as industries are replaced or relocated. Seventy years ago, the commanding heights of the UK economy - characterised by the coal, iron and steel and ship-building industries - were located in regions now more closely associated with economic decline, such as Tyneside and South Wales. Over the last decade waves of unemployment have hit particular industries and regions hard. It has not always been the manufacturing sector which has lost the most jobs. Over 100,000 jobs in the financial services sector have been lost since the onset of the last recession *[16]*. Barclays Bank and National Westminster Bank have announced that at least 7,200 jobs would be lost between them during 1994 as a result of new technologies replacing people, and rationalisation of existing arrangements to reduce operating costs *[16]*.

The Government has not coped with these shifts in a socially and environmentally responsible manner *[17]*. A far more innovative, integrated and enlightened approach will be needed in the future. Examples of how it might be done are already available. One option is to develop conversion

"...One option is to develop conversion strategies which aim to transform polluting or resource-profligate companies into environmentally acceptable alternatives..."

strategies which aim to transform polluting or resource-profligate companies into environmentally acceptable alternatives.

In the past, trade unionists have examined such strategies in response to mass redundancies. In 1976, workers at Lucas Aerospace, a company which relied heavily on the defence industry for contracts, drew up a plan to divert the company's resources into the development of more socially-useful products to avoid further redundancies [18]. Five alternative product areas were covered in the plan - medical equipment, including a 'design for the disabled' unit; alternative energy technologies, including windmills using Lucas' expertise in aerodynamics; transport technologies such as the development of a combined road-rail vehicle; braking systems; and ocean-based technologies. More recently the European Commission established a funding programme called KONVER [19], to assist areas dependent on the defence industry to diversify their economies. Projects that can be funded by the programme include a variety of training initiatives, conversion strategies, feasibility studies, aiding the development of small- and medium-sized businesses, and temporary funding for posts during conversion.

In Japan state support for industrial restructuring is highly sophisticated and well-established. A range of policy options are available for any development programme - including research and development grants, soft loans for investment and export credits. These examples suggest some of the components of an integrated and strategically-based environmental and economic policy which could bring government and industry into partnership.

The geography of change towards sustainable development is also important. Job gains and losses at a local level need to be put into context by overall employment effects at the national level. However, small net job gains at a national level can hide very significant employment gains and losses at a local level. It is equally important to consider the international impacts of such policy shifts. However, these impacts are far from clear [20]. One potential impact that has been recognised is that where countries fall behind in the drive to tighten environmental regulation, they risk losing competitiveness [21,22]. It is, however, worth noting that other international policy measures, such as trade liberalisation and unregulated capital flows, can be expected to have far more significant impacts upon the distribution of employment, than changes in environmental policy.

In order to get a clearer idea of the opportunities for job creation through sustainable development, sector-based case studies addressing pollution control, transport, energy, resource use and agriculture are presented below. In each case, existing research on the economic implications of environmental policies is reviewed, with particular attention to employment.

Pollution Control

*"...if the **Polluter Pays Principle** was honoured throughout the economy, employment in the environmental control industry would be 200,000 higher..."*

Manufacturing industry is fundamentally important in every developed economy and increasingly important in developing countries. It is also a central cause of the environmental problems faced today, as summed up by the European Commission in its Fifth Environmental Action Programme:

"in its exploitation of natural resources, consumption of energy, production processes and generation of both pollution and wastes, the industrial sector is among the principal causes of environmental deterioration" [23, p.28].

In the past, governments, commerce and industry have treated environmental objectives and the objectives of manufacturing industry as at best, conflicting and at worst, mutually exclusive. Increasingly, however, those views are changing. The Earth Summit of 1992 promoted the need for environmental, social and economic objectives to be integrated and this objective is now incorporated into the Treaty on European Union [24]. The Fifth Environment Action Programme noted that industry was beginning to suffer from the environmental damage it had caused:

"Insofar as the environmental consequences of industrial activity may exceed the tolerance level of the natural resource base it can limit or block further industrial development in a locality or region" [23, p.28].

The potential to achieve environmental, social and economic objectives simultaneously is exemplified by recent research on the employment

21

"...firms affected by tighter pollution control standards can reap longer term economic benefits from environmental protection..."

impacts of pollution control policies completed by Cambridge Econometrics. The Labour Party recently cited a general figure from this research of 682,000 jobs being created by *"higher environmental standards"* [25]. This figure, comes from one combined scenario, which includes the effects of a carbon tax (a measure that the Labour Party has now rejected as policy) alongside specific investments. It is more useful to examine the various measures separately.

Estimates of job creation resulting from certain aspects of pollution control have been produced by Cambridge Econometrics. Using computer modelling techniques it was found that if the *Polluter Pays Principle* was honoured throughout the economy, employment in the environmental control industry would be 200,000 higher than the predicted base level in 2005, with consequent beneficial income, expenditure and fiscal effects on the rest of the economy [26]. Alternatively, a major investment programme to improve water quality was forecast to create 696,000 additional direct and indirect jobs by the year 2005 using the same modelling techniques [26].

Yet despite policy declarations and initiatives from business groupings such as the International Chamber of Commerce and its offspring, the World Industry Council on the Environment [27, 28, 29], and mounting evidence, much industrial activity remains unchanged. Demands on industry to reduce pollution are still cited as an example of how environmental protection threatens jobs. In reality, most firms affected by tighter pollution control standards can reap longer term economic benefits from environmental protection rather than just bear short term costs.

Are compliance costs significant?

Although companies, particularly in the manufacturing sector, will face additional costs, the cost of complying with environmental regulation varies between countries, industrial sectors and even subsectors. Processing industries generally experience higher compliance costs than component manufacturers and assemblers. In the US, for example, four industries - chemicals, petroleum, pulp and paper and primary metals - account for almost 75 per cent of pollution control expenditures in the manufacturing sector in 1991. These same industries are also responsible for a disproportionate share of pollution and hazardous waste; yet only account for 22 per cent of the 'value added' by the manufacturing sector [21].

But it is important to note that compliance costs are not a major share of total costs for any industry, even in countries with comparatively high environmental standards. In the previous example the four polluting sectors only devoted 15 per cent of their *capital expenditure* to pollution control - compared to just 3.2 per cent for all other manufacturing sectors in 1991. This amounts to 4.85 per cent of the *value added* by the four polluting industries, compared to an average of 1.72 per cent of manufacturing as a whole [21]. The UK's chemical, metals and food processing industries only spent between 1.15 and 1.37 per cent of their *turnover* on pollution control in 1988. For engineering the figure was 0.3 per cent and for fuel processing 0.4 per cent [30].

Nonetheless, small shifts in marginal costs can be significant for individual companies. So how do these direct costs relate to employment? The most common argument suggesting that such costs lead to job losses is that firms, as a direct consequence of environmental compliance costs, will close factories or make workers redundant. However, a survey

"...In a survey of plant closures in the UK, environmental costs were cited as an important factor in only one out of 193 cases..."

covering the European Union estimates that where compliance costs are less that two per cent of turnover - the case in all the industries considered above - they are unlikely to result in plant closure.

Other evidence supports the argument that such plant closures are unlikely. Research in countries such as Germany, Sweden and the United States [31] indicates that the adverse employment effects of plant closures attributable to environmental policy have been very limited. In a survey of plant closures in the UK, environmental costs were cited as an important factor in only one out of 193 cases. This represented 0.2 per cent of the total job losses covered by the survey. The real and significant causes of redundancies included structural shift in demand, recession, import penetration and fluctuations in exchange rates [32].

Plants that have allegedly closed for environmental reasons are often small, old and marginal. They would probably have closed anyway. At most, environmental regulations have simply accelerated the timing of already inevitable closure [33]. For example, the Avenue coke works near Chesterfield, owned by Coal Products Ltd (CPL), faced costly demands from the National Rivers Authority to clean up its management of liquid effluents in 1992. Yet the closure of the works, in 1993, was, according to CPL's Managing Director, caused mainly by declining domestic demand for smokeless fuel and the need to bring coal from further away to maintain supplies of sufficient quality [34]. The Engineering Employers Federation in the UK replied to claims by firms in the metals sectors that environmental regulations had led to closure or a drop in profitability by saying that:

"the real determining factor is the strength of the UK economy and the need to be competitive in world markets. Environmental expenditure is

"it is the failure of companies to clean up their acts which is the surest way of losing jobs"

often just the last straw landing on people's backs" [35].

In many cases environmentally aware management of firms can avoid such situations. When improvements in environmental performance are required by government and the public, those firms that fail to act early and fall behind their competitors find that when the problem finally catches up with them it is far bigger and has more serious consequences. In other words, the reverse of the oft-asserted dictum is true - **bad environmental management often costs jobs.** As one union representative put it: *"it is the failure of companies to clean up their acts which is the surest way of losing jobs"* [36].

In response to the suggestion by some of its member firms that deadlines for compliance with environmental regulations be postponed in the UK, the Engineering Employers Federation has said that such an extension may simply: *"give some firms more rope to hang themselves with"* [35]

Environmental Innovation

Importantly, environmental protection provides firms with potential benefits as well as costs. These benefits can be "both broad and deep" [37], affecting many different aspects of a firm's operations, often in a fundamental manner. They present opportunities for the very firms who are being regulated to create badly-needed jobs. Indeed, it should be noted that some of the compliance costs themselves are in the form of new jobs, for example in monitoring or managing waste flows [21, 31].

Most importantly, environmental regulation can stimulate technological or management innovation to find more efficient ways of ensuring compliance. This carries several benefits for firms. Improvements in

"...policies aimed specifically at stimulating innovation showed no association with successful projects. However, regulations were positively related to increased innovation..."

the level and nature of research and development (R&D) can occur as firms seek creative solutions to environmental problems [38]. Long-established industries, in particular, can benefit from this spur to innovate [39]. Where firms do successfully innovate for compliance they can gain both a renewed competitive advantage and potential new markets for their innovation [39]. Such responses to environmental regulation can increase job security and create new jobs.

Governments around the world recognise the need for industry to innovate, particularly as a means of breaking out of recessionary cycles. A study of the influence of government policy on industrial innovation in five countries including Japan and the UK found that policies aimed specifically at stimulating innovation showed no association with successful projects. However, regulations were positively related to increased innovation [40]. In the case of environmental regulations, the survey found that in many cases there was a "reservoir of technology" which lay under-utilized and could be tapped for rapid improvements.

A UK survey of cleaner technology developments provided several examples to support this finding. One firm cited in the study developed a prototype technology for recycling phenol waste in 1984, which was forecast to give a £17,500 per year saving in energy costs against a capital investment of £250,000, only to shelve the idea. Several years later the firm reached its legal discharge limit and subsequently completed the development process and installed the technology [41].

Further benefits for both the firm and employment levels can arise from 'spin-off' innovation - technological developments which are triggered by regulations but are not specifically necessary for compliance with

**"...environmental regulations present opportunities
to increase profitability..."**

them. A review of such benefits in the chemical industry of the United States found examples including the development of new product formulations, new catalysts for distilling crude oil and better process monitoring techniques, which increased yields and reduced health and safety risks [39].

Cutting Costs

Perhaps the most appealing benefit for firms is that environmental regulations present opportunities to increase profitability. The implications for employment are also significant because profitability is not increased at the expense of jobs, but by cutting other costs. Developing and adopting cleaner technology can bring a reduction in three other types of cost - those for raw materials, energy and waste disposal.

In the case of waste disposal, regulation has begun to increase disposal charges to a level which accounts, at least in part, for the environmental costs involved. As a result, waste producers can save increasingly large sums by producing less waste or by eradicating the discharges altogether. Two regional waste minimisation schemes in the UK have emphasised this by identifying potential annual savings of £13 million for just 25 companies [42].

Such changes also bring indirect benefits - including reducing the potential for exposure to liability from environmental damage caused by waste and better relations with local communities and customers. For example, Express Foods dairy, in Appleby-in-Westmorland, was fined £25,000 for an ammonia spill into the River Eden in 1987 which killed thousands of fish. It also had to pay £112,000 for restocking the river. In response, the factory established a waste reduction programme which saved the firm £80,000 in the first year alone. Since then an investment of £100,000 in in-process recycling to reduce waste generation has been paid back in under a year and the firm estimates annual savings of £175,000 [43].

Process efficiency is very often increased by the drive to minimize waste production. A process which uses less raw materials and energy is also likely to produce less waste. Other developments, including recovery and re-use of materials, recycling process water, in-process energy recovery units and material replacement, all have economic benefits that can often repay the initial investment within a timespan of months or up to a couple of years [44].

Two waste minimisation schemes in the UK have identified projects with financial savings for the firms concerned. Over 69 per cent of these schemes either cost nothing to implement or have payback times of less than one year [42]. The Blue Circle cement company covered investment costs of over £200,000 on a kiln management system which reduced emissions of nitrogen oxides by more than half, as well as increasing fuel efficiency, in less than three months [45].

Despite such potential benefits, many industrialists oppose environmental regulations on the grounds that they are unattainable. But such arguments are often exposed as mere prevarication. In Germany, a decade ago, industry opposed what they saw as unattainable new laws controlling nitrogen oxides emissions. However, at that time firms in Japan were already achieving the new standards. After importing Japanese know-how initially, Germany developed its own manufacturing base and now exports the relevant technology **and** its industries are

"...although waste costs UK industry £2.6 billion per year, some 44 per cent of UK firms do not keep track of waste costs..."

more energy-efficient as a result [46].

Firms need to change their outlook if the opportunities for creating jobs as part of a dynamic sustainable economy are to be taken. Vitally, companies should seek to integrate environmental objectives into all aspects of their activities rather consider them as an 'add-on'. The 'software' as well as the 'hardware' of business activity needs to change. A recent report from the consulting firm Arthur D Little noted that even the firms most active in addressing environmental concerns must make a break from a functional perspective, dealing with the environment through management systems, to a genuine business perspective, seeking the strategic opportunities in environmental management [47]. For example, until recently, few firms audited the environmental impacts of their operations: and indeed many still fail to do so. A recent study [48] revealed that, although waste costs UK industry £2.6 billion per year, some 44 per cent of UK firms do not keep track of waste costs, and over half have no plans for waste minimisation. Only when they have adequate detailed information can firms start to realise the potential cost savings.

Regulation and employment

It would be wrong to suggest that potential job gains will inevitably be realised, no matter what form of regulation is used. It is essential that policy makers choose appropriate regulatory instruments. For example regulatory tools such as Best Available Technique Not Entailing Excessive Costs (BATNEEC), because of the emphasis on costs, still tend to lock industries into established technologies and those tend to be inadequate 'end-of-pipe' solutions. Under such a regime, existing plant will rarely be replaced before the end of its operating life. The danger is that such measures create a disincentive to fundamental longer-term change [12, 49] - the sort of change which is vital if sustainable development is to be achieved.

As advances in effluent monitoring and information processing continue, and the need to link environmental regulations to environmental constraints becomes more urgent, so regulation based upon achieving environmental quality can become the norm. This process, although implicit in some Governmental initiatives, is still in its infancy in the UK and EU. When appropriate regulations are reinforced by market incentives to go beyond compliance, and by schemes to aid small and medium firms to make the necessary transitions, they can force firms to reap the rewards of cleaner technology and, in the process, secure existing jobs and create new ones.

Another argument used against introducing stringent pollution control measures is that industry will migrate to countries where pollution control laws are more relaxed. Although some transnational firms undoubtedly exploit, and indeed even lobby to maintain the differences between national pollution control laws once established in a country [50], a review of foreign direct investment in Mexico, Eire, Romania and Taiwan found that only in the case of US asbestos firms' relocation in Mexico was environmental regulation a significant factor in the firms' location decisions [51]. Labour costs are a far more important consideration.

It is clear that improving environmental protection by tightly controlling industrial pollution can have a positive impact on employment levels. This is most clearly seen over the long-term. As the International Confederation of Free Trade Unions stated:

"...the global market for environmental services and for traditional pollution control equipment was $200 billion in 1990, with the potential to grow to $300 billion in the year 2000...."

"in the future the pressure will be for real, lasting, socially useful and individually satisfying jobs. In the future the companies best able to ensure job security will be those who perform well environmentally and economically" [52].

But, as outlined above, there are also real short- and medium-term increases in employment opportunities if firms and government embrace comprehensive and integrated environmental management. A recent report on Industry and Environment from the House of Lords endorsed the European Commission's aim that the Government should use environmental policy to make industry more competitive [53].

The Pollution Control Industry

In fact, pollution control industries themselves are important employers. The Organisation for Economic Co-operation and Development estimated the global market for environmental services and for traditional pollution control equipment at $200 billion in 1990, with the potential to grow to $300 billion in the year 2000 [54]. A US Government study placed the 1992 market at $295 billion worldwide, with potential to grow to $426 billion by 1997 [21].

These markets create and support jobs. Figures for employment in Germany and France in the 1980s suggest that 1.7 per cent of the total workforce in these countries was engaged in environmental protection [31]. More recently, it has been estimated that 1.3 per cent of the total employment in the European Union was supported by environmental expenditure [30]. In the United States, the proportion is estimated to be as high as 2.5 per cent. An analysis of US pollution control expenditure

"...UK expenditure of £3,846 million
in 1992 may have supported some 115,000 jobs..."

suggests that outlays of roughly $100 billion in 1988 supported or created almost three million direct and indirect jobs [55]. Many of these are high-wage, skilled jobs. Applying this ratio to the UK expenditure of £3,846 million in 1992 [30, 56] would suggest that some 115,380 jobs were supported. This may be an over-estimate, as this industry is not as developed in the UK as it is in the US. More generally, employment in the sector is forecast to increase dramatically over the next few years. One study predicted a 72 per cent rise in employment in the European environmental protection industry from 1992 to 2000, excluding exports to non-EU countries [30]. Extrapolating from the estimates given above, this suggests that perhaps 80,000 more jobs may arise in the UK industry.

As the environmental goods and services market has become established, so competition within it has increased. Industrialised countries accounted for 80 per cent of this global market in 1990 and are likely to continue to dominate it for the next decade [54]. The United States, in particular, represents 40 per cent of the global market for these goods and services [21]. The countries of the European Union make up roughly 28 per cent of the market [57]. However, developing countries, particularly fast-growing East Asian countries, such as South Korea and Taiwan [55], are already significant purchasers of some environmental technologies. Thailand, for example, has a pollution control equipment market worth US $210 million which is expected to reach US $1.5 billion by 2000 [58]. The countries of central and eastern Europe are also important growing markets.

Despite the size of the global market, just three countries take over half of it. A survey by the German Federal Ministry of Research and Technology in 1992 showed that Germany, the United States and Japan had leapt ahead of other competitors to take advantage of the

"...The countries with the largest environmental control industries have some of the strictest environmental regulations in the world. Their firms have benefited as other countries have inevitably had to raise their environmental standards..."

opportunities to export environmental technology. The UK's share was so small that it did not even rate a mention [59].

As one of the world's leading industrialised nations one would expect the UK to have an established environmental control industry. A recent Government-sponsored report of the industry's export record estimated that the industry generates a £234 million trade surplus annually [60]. But this falls far short of the potential. Although the UK has established industries in a few areas of environmental technology - in particular water treatment [60] - as highlighted by a recent House of Lords report [53], we have consistently tended to miss out on the opportunities which have arisen. The UK has therefore also missed out on the jobs that could have been generated as a result.

This country has an excellent track record in scientific discovery and technological application. Flue Gas Desulphurisation (FGD), was invented in the UK. But German firms refined and marketed FGD in Europe, and retrained redundant ship-builders, notably welders, in its manufacture [61, 62]. The main reason for this is that every fossil-fuel power station in Germany was required by law to adopt the Best Available Technique to reduce emissions of the pollutants which cause acid rain. This proved to mean fitting FGD. In contrast, the UK has required only two power stations to fit the technology. This is just one example of how strict regulation has been a driving force for economic success.

The countries with the largest environmental control industries - Germany, the United States and Japan - have some of the strictest environmental regulations in the world. Their firms have benefited as other countries have inevitably had to raise their environmental standards.

"...In the UK, weak regulation and ineffective enforcement have prevented innovative firms from developing and creating more jobs..."

In the countries of the Pacific Rim, nascent environmental control industries are set to benefit from national programmes of environmental expenditure [21].

In the UK, weak regulation and ineffective enforcement, combined with underfunded and piecemeal support programmes for the environment control industry, have prevented innovative firms from developing and creating more jobs. Even so, a recent survey of firms in the UK environmental control industry found that UK and European environmental legislation was the main customer stimulus to buy environmental technologies [63]. As the managing director of one firm said:

"If the UK enforces decent environmental legislation, it gives a great stimulus for us to develop the technology and then use our home market as a base for expansion into Europe" [64].

Despite the record of lost opportunities, the Government and industry still have a chance to get in early on the next transformation in the market - to cleaner technologies. In the past the environmental control industry has been dominated by the concept of pollution control rather than pollution prevention. Environmental technologies were and still are predominantly end-of-pipe, 'bolt on', appliances designed to treat wastes produced by industrial processes. In the majority of cases, the waste is only converted into another comparatively less harmful form of pollution. If sustainable development is to be achieved, such an approach is no longer tenable [65].

**"...cleaner technologies have the potential
to generate more jobs than conventional
pollution control..."**

Cleaning up

Cleaner technologies use less energy and raw materials and produce less waste. They offer both environmental and economic benefits. Although barriers to the development and diffusion of cleaner technologies still exist [13], they will increasingly dominate industrial development as governments regulate to meet environmental goals. This will lead to radical changes in the environmental control industry. But, yet again, firms from those countries which have integrated pollution prevention into actual policy, will be best placed to exploit the potential [21].

Although the concept of cleaner technology has been around for over a decade and the commercial potential is high, development efforts are still in their early stages. The forecasts of the environmental control market cited above do not take account of cleaner technologies. The potential global markets may be substantially bigger than even the more optimistic estimates.

As cleaner production processes and technologies become more widely used, some sections of the environmental control industry will suffer, while others gain. As demand for 'end-of-pipe' technology falls, firms which produce such equipment - for example for scrubbing pollutants out of gaseous discharges or treating industrial waste water - will need to adjust. However, other firms will have increased opportunities, such as those which monitor pollutants in waste streams. In a sustainable economy the high cost of energy, raw materials and emissions will mean that firms will need to monitor their environmental performance very carefully. There will also be greater stimulus to innovation. Overall, cleaner technologies have the potential to generate more jobs than conventional pollution control [21].

"...The goal for government and industry working in partnership, therefore must be to exploit the opportunities presented by the transition to sustainable development.."

The UK has the potential to exploit this transition. In common with the rest of Europe, small and medium sized firms play a vital role in this sector in the UK. The OECD estimates that over half of the output of Europe's environmental protection industry is provided by firms employing less than 50 people [54]. In the UK, despite lax environmental enforcement and the recession, both of which have reduced demand, many of the specialised firms designing and manufacturing monitoring equipment have continued to create jobs. For example, Codel International, based in Bakewell, manufactures stack emission monitoring equipment and has increased its workforce from 30 to 48 in the last two years [66]. PCME (Europe) Ltd of Huntingdon produces dust emissions monitoring equipment and since 1990, when it employed just two people, it has created 19 more jobs [67]. Southern Science Ltd is an environmental consultancy which also produces a mobile laboratory for environmental analysis of contaminated land and has expanded its workforce from 100 to 140 in the last five years [68].

The goal for government and industry working in partnership, therefore must be to exploit the opportunities presented by the transition to sustainable development. For the UK, the question is will we miss out again or will the Government act to channel industrial activity in the right direction? Unfortunately the Government continues to take a wholly unsatisfactory piece-meal approach, apparently content to dabble in one policy measure at a time in order to stimulate the development and uptake of cleaner technologies [69].

In other countries, such as the United States, several policies are operated together and benefit from the driving force of environmental regulation. By contrast, in the UK, incentive schemes are introduced at the same

> **"...The UK Government has the opportunity to create and support jobs in the environmental control industry. By doing so it would not only be protecting the environment but exploiting the country's considerable potential for innovation.."**

time as deregulation is being sought. This haphazard and contradictory approach undermines one of the most important measures of sustainable development planning: namely the integration of environmental and economic priorities. If environmental and economic policies are not integrated, industry will find it increasingly difficult to meet the challenges ahead and the UK will miss out on environmental technology jobs again. In comparison, Japan launched its New Sunshine Programme last year, aimed at developing cleaner technologies over 27 years [46] (longer than the 18-year time-frame considered in the UK's Sustainable Development Strategy!).

Conclusion

The UK Government has the opportunity to create and support jobs in the environmental control industry. By doing so it would not only be protecting the environment but exploiting the country's considerable potential for innovation. Measures to ensure that the UK industry can take its share of the growing market could provide an estimated 80,000 additional jobs in the UK by the year 2000.

If the opportunity is to be taken, the Government must reform its policies and increase its support for the industry. Environmental regulation should be strengthened and enforcement tightened, but in ways which encourage innovation. Cleaning up provides firms with economic opportunities and costs savings. Modelling suggests that properly implementing the polluter pays principle could increase employment by 200,000 by 2005, while substantial investment in water quality improvements could create almost 700,000 jobs over the same period.

Transport

The motor manufacturing industry, having been one of the major driving forces that has shaped the global economy over the last few decades, is now recognised as a major cause of the world's environmental problems. The products of the motor industry - mainly passenger cars - are globally the single largest source of anthropogenic air pollution. For example, road traffic is the fastest-growing source of greenhouse gases which makes it a priority target in the race against climate change. Some 14 per cent of the world's carbon dioxide emissions come from road transport [70] - in the UK the figure is 20 per cent [71].

Motor vehicles are a major source of toxic pollutants which pose significant threats to human health and the environment. Vehicle emissions in the UK account for 53 per cent of nitrogen oxides (NOx), 90 per cent of carbon monoxide, 46 per cent of volatile organic compounds and 47 per cent of black smoke [71]. The growth in emissions of NOx from traffic has been associated with a doubling of reported cases of asthma [72]. Benzene in petrol is a cause of cancer [73], and diesel engine emissions of PM10s (compound particulates under 10 micrometres in diameter) are estimated to kill 3,000 people a year in the UK alone [74].

But the impact of road transport goes beyond emissions. The building of new roads destroys large areas of countryside and open spaces. At least 35 Sites of Special Scientific Interest, Britain's key wildlife sites, are threatened by Government road building plans [75]. A recent survey found that in South East England alone, some 200 important wildlife sites were under threat from proposals for road building or widening [76].

Motor manufacturing is deeply embedded in western economies. Nine of the world's top 30 industrial groups are motor manufacturers. The industry is estimated to be responsible, directly and indirectly, for nearly two per cent of the working population of the countries of the European Union [77]. Yet those jobs may become increasingly insecure as action is taken by governments to promote sustainable development and abate urgent global environmental threats, such as climate change. Motor manufacturers are belatedly embracing measures such as life-cycle analysis, fuel efficiency and emission controls, but they know that their future ultimately depends upon being able to remain profitable in a world with less demand for car travel.

The pronouncements of Margaret Thatcher, and politicians from all sides of the political spectrum on the forward march of "the great car economy" are completely out of touch with present realities. For example, Volvo now sees its own long-term future as a market leader in urban rapid transport systems, not cars [78]. In the transition to sustainable transport the ability of firms and regions to move from solely making and selling cars to producing vehicles for advanced public transport systems is vital if employment impacts are to be minimized. In the Midlands, for example, Coventry has shown how engineering skills in the transport sector can be transferred: during this century production has progressed from bicycle manufacture to motorcycles to cars.

Overlaps and similarities between the skills needed in car and rail industries, and the capacity to shift from one to another, have been highlighted recently by the Institute for Ecological Economic Research

"...research findings expose road building to be poor value for money as a job creator..."

in Wuppertal, Germany [55]. Additionally, the ability of car manufacturers to create jobs has waned with the introduction of increasingly automated assembly lines. A recent report has exposed the failure of the new Toyota plant in Derbyshire to significantly boost the local economy and create the numbers of jobs forecast when the factory was proposed [79].

Two other employment issues are raised in debates over transport policy - job creation through road building and the contribution of motor manufacturers to dynamic economies which create and maintain jobs. On both these counts, sustainable transport developments, based on a reduced need to travel and the promotion of public transport, cycling and walking, as well as improved vehicle technologies, can provide a greater boost to job creation opportunities.

Transport infrastructure - building jobs?

Given the dominance of road transport in most industrialised countries, it is not surprising that governments rely on building more roads when looking for policies to create jobs and stimulate the economy. Yet employment policies based on this conventional approach, such as the European Union proposals for a trans-European road network [80], ignore research findings which expose road building to be poor value for money as a job creator. A recent study by the German Road League and the construction union IG Bau Steine Erden showed that investing DM100 billion on roads would yield only 1,201 to 1,630 person-years of employment as compared to about 1,880 job-years in railway construction or 1,992 in local public transport such as light rail track construction [55, 81]. In other words, developing a sustainable transport infrastructure creates more jobs, as well as helping control the adverse

"...if £500 million was directed at investments in the rail network, between 3,000 and 8,150 more jobs would be created than if the money were spent on road building.."

environmental impacts of road building. Moreover, these figures do not include the jobs created in operating public transport systems.

Because of variations in the classification of spending on different modes of transport by Government statisticians it is virtually impossible to calculate exactly how much the UK government currently invests in roads and railways. However, Government spending on roads for 1992-3 was estimated at about £3 billion [82]. The bulk of this was spent on new construction and structural maintenance. UK Government 'support' for the railways (including London Underground and light rail but excluding borrowing approvals) was around £2 billion.

Transport 2000 recently presented an alternative government transport budget which involved no net increase in spending. In this alternative budget, £593 million was transferred from new road construction to rail and rail freight. It can be estimated, using the German figures cited above, that if £500 million of this was directed at investments in the rail network, between 3,000 and 8,150 more jobs would be created than if the money were spent on road building [83]. The alternative budget also included a transfer of £450 million from road construction expenditure to light rail. If £400 million of this was directed at new light rail construction, an estimated 3,475 to 7,590 additional jobs would be created [83]. Combining these figures gives 6,475-15,740 additional jobs.

These findings are backed up by a study in the UK which compared a number of major investment schemes in terms of price-per-job. Transport schemes included in the survey repeatedly showed that rail projects were better value for money as job creators *(See Table 1)*. In other words, adopting sustainable transport options brings more employment as well as higher environmental returns on each pound invested.

Finally, the argument that road building brings prosperity and jobs to the areas it serves is also unproven. There is a dearth of large-scale primary research on the issue of employment generated in economies by road investments and the work completed has often failed to support the argument [84]. This lack of empirical evidence is highlighted by a recent lobbying document issued by the British Roads Federation (BRF) in the face of cuts in the UK roads programme [85]. In a crude and fundamentally flawed analysis the BRF ignored the economic and employment benefits of alternative policies [86] and resorted to using a model which effectively designed out some of the key weaknesses in its argument [87].

Table 1:
The financial cost of job creation in selected infrastructure projects

Project	Cost per job (£)
Energy efficiency	8,750-17,500
Building 100,000 new homes	20,000-40,000
East London Line	34,000
Northern Line Refurbishment	34,000
Midland Main-line Electrification	34,000
West Coast Main-line Upgrade	35,000
Jubilee Line Extension	50,000
New Forth Road Bridge	65,000
East Coast Motorway	66,000
M6 Widening	66,000
M1 Widening	67,000
East London River Crossing (Road)	68,000
M25 Widening	78,000

Source: Sunday Times, 25th October 1992, figures provided by Cambridge Econometrics.

"...European Transport Ministers have agreed that road building is unlikely to attract business to an area..."

Roads and the Economy

A main strand of the argument that road building boosts the economy is that firms' transport costs are reduced. Yet transport costs account for a small portion of a company's total costs. One of the main reasons is that transport costs on average account for a small proportion of a firm's total costs: normally in the order of five to ten per cent and only up to 20 per cent for distribution services [88]. According to a recent survey, transport costs represent on average only around two per cent of firms' sales revenue in the UK [89]. In addition a significant proportion of these costs are terminal costs - incurred in loading and unloading, and therefore cannot be reduced by road improvements. European Transport Ministers have agreed that road building is unlikely to attract business to an area through reducing transport costs:

"location decisions are influenced less by the cost of transport than by other factors such as fixed costs, particularly labour costs. By and large businesses do not consider transport costs to be an important factor" [90].

One of the main employment effects of strategic road building is to redistribute rather than create jobs. In fact, redistribution can often include relocation and corporate reorganisation with consequential job losses. The major effect of new roads on the brewing industry, for example, has been one of centralisation which facilitates economies of scale and hence the shedding of jobs [91]. Warehousing and distribution firms have also been shown to cut jobs as a result of reorganisation or consolidation following road building schemes [92].

At the national level, as Figure 3 illustrates, the difference between car kilometres per unit wealth in Japan and Switzerland, compared to the

"...the major factor cited by potential employers for not locating in Docklands was the area's inaccessibility by public transport..."

UK, makes it clear that no direct causal link exists between them. Evidence is available, however, which supports the argument that investments in public transport will be better at securing and creating jobs and stimulating wider economic activities than road transport investments. For example, during the recent attempt to revitalise the economy of east London through massive public and private capital expenditure in the Docklands area, the London Docklands Development Corporation (LDDC) allocated £2 billion - 25 per cent of its spending - to road building and just 4 per cent of that amount to a new light rail system. In the first six years local firms - which employed 27,000 people before the Docklands programme began - had made over 50 per cent of their workers redundant as a result of LDDC's compulsory purchase of land and the disruption caused by development activities. Even with new employers moving into the area there was a net employment loss of 5,000 jobs [93]. A survey conducted two years later found that the major factor cited by potential employers for not locating in Docklands was the area's inaccessibility by public transport [94]. LDDC's failure to invest adequately in public transport was therefore a contributing factor to the net loss of jobs in this local economy.

In urban areas, restricting car access and pedestrianisation has increased security of employment in the retail sector. The Organisation for Economic Co-operation and Development (OECD) in an international survey found that only two per cent of pedestrianisation schemes led to a fall in retail turnover. Some 49 per cent of the schemes recorded upward trends in turnover, mostly of around 25 per cent. The OECD concluded that *"pedestrianisation is an economic success"* [95].

The employment impacts of road transport policies also include costs as well as alleged benefits. The CBI has estimated that traffic congestion

Figure 3: Wealth and Road Transport in Different Countries

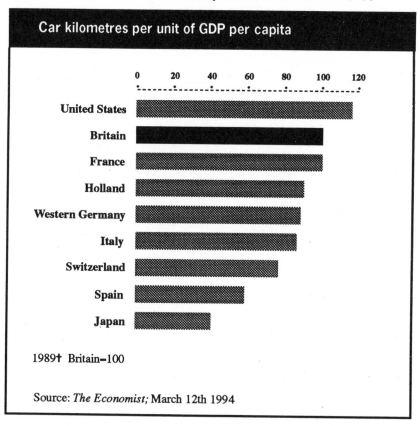

Car kilometres per unit of GDP per capita

1989† Britain=100

Source: *The Economist;* March 12th 1994

costs UK industry some £15 billion annually [96]. Traffic congestion
has been estimated to cost the United States some $100 billion in lost
productivity. In Japan, traffic congestion on the roads is threatening

47

jobs by undermining the country's famed 'just-in-time' delivery system, in which carefully scheduled trucks make continuous, small deliveries so that industrial and commercial enterprises can avoid keeping large inventories on site. Ironically, this delivery system - credited by many for Japan's efficiency in car manufacturing - further contributes to traffic congestion, threatening to choke road capacity for the industry's own products [97]. Increasingly, congestion is also becoming a significant cost in the air transport sector. The International Air Traffic Association estimates that Europe loses $10 billion each year to air traffic bottle-necks [55].

The motor industry's profligate consumption of fuel not only has a high environmental cost but also has implications for employment. Dependence on oil to fuel road transport strains many nations' balance of payments, making economies vulnerable to swings in the world price of oil. Regional and local economies are also affected. A recent study in Los Angeles shows that 85 cents of every local dollar spent on petrol leaves the regional economy, much of it leaving the country as well. In contrast, out of every dollar that buys a fare on public transport, an estimated 80 cents goes toward transport workers' wages. The study found that the circulation of those 80 cents in the local economy generated more than $3.80 in goods and services in the region [98].

Conclusion

Following sustainable transport strategies can provide benefits for employment at national, regional and local levels. As road-building programmes are scrapped, measures to reduce the growth in car numbers introduced and the benefits of rail transport exploited, both private and public sectors have an opportunity to maximise potential employment benefits. A key measure to reduce car use and reduce transport emissions would be to further increase road fuel duty, above the Government's agreed increases. The substantial potential employment advantages of this policy are considered below in the discussion of tax reform.

A transformation of the transport sector, away from the strangle-hold of the 'car economy' and towards sustainability, is essential. Substantial investment in reorienting production and retraining workforces will be needed. Public expenditure should be shifted away from road-building to investments in railways and public transport that, estimates suggest, could create up to 15,700 additional jobs in 1995.

Energy

"...economic success is associated with high energy efficiency..."

Energy lies at the heart of the sustainable development paradigm. On one hand it literally fuels the global economy and is essential to meeting peoples' needs. On the other hand, the supply technologies which currently dominate the energy sector make a substantial contribution to the current environmental crisis. Investing in energy efficiency is a proven strategy for meeting environmental, social and economic objectives. As well as offering reductions in atmospheric pollution, lower fuel bills for consumers, and increased comfort for low-income householders, investment in energy efficiency also creates jobs.

At the scale of national economies a study by the International Energy Agency indicates a strong relationship between economic growth and energy intensity [99]. But the positive correlation is not that which one might at first assume. The IEA study found that those economies where energy intensity is high grow slowly, while those where energy intensity is low grow faster (see Figure 4). In other words, economic success is associated with high energy efficiency and not simply with increased supply of energy.

Numerous studies have been completed which highlight the role that demand-side management (DSM) - reducing users' demands for energy through conservation and efficiency measures - can play in job creation [100].

Employment can be generated in manufacture, delivery and installation, as well as in assessing the need for energy efficiency products. A large

Figure 4: Energy Intensity and Economic Growth

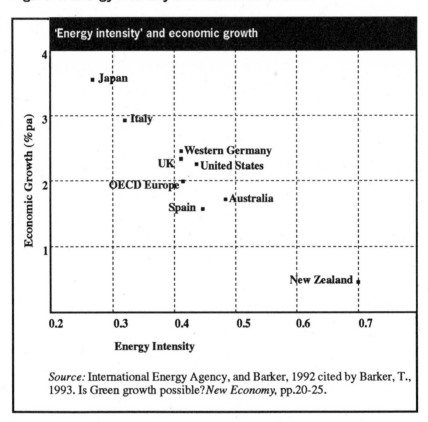

Source: International Energy Agency, and Barker, 1992 cited by Barker, T., 1993. Is Green growth possible? *New Economy*, pp.20-25.

"...A large proportion of these jobs are unskilled and semi-skilled, and likely to be concentrated in areas of high unemployment..."

proportion of these jobs are unskilled and semi-skilled, and likely to be concentrated in areas of high unemployment where many of the buildings requiring remedial work are situated. Job creation benefits like these are of tremendous importance in a country like Britain with very high unemployment rates in decaying urban centres. In addition to the jobs created directly there are substantial indirect or 'knock-on' employment benefits. Firstly, those now employed will consume additional goods and services - so more employment results from the economic 'multiplier effect'. Secondly, money saved on fuel costs is spent on other goods and services - the 'respending effect'.

Table 2: Job Generation by Investment in Energy Efficiency

Study	Investment (£bn gross)	Job-years created	Net cost per job-year (£)	Programme length (yrs)
ACE/ERL	15.5	500,000	23,000	10
	38.0	1,223,000	23,000	20
ERR	62.0	2,500,000	17,000	30
Fraunhofer	14.6	594,000	16,500	38
Lousiana	0.22	12,600	9,300	10
Boardman	16.50	970,000	9,000	13

Source: Taylor, L. 1992. Employment aspects of energy efficiency. In Christie, I. and Ritchie, N. (eds)Energy efficiency: the policy agenda for the 1990s. London: Policy Studies Institute.

"...an affordable and manageable ten-year national energy conservation programme, directed at reducing space heating in buildings in all sectors would create 500,000 job-years of work..."

Saving jobs - energy efficiency

A study by Environmental Resources Limited (ERL) for the Association for the Conservation of Energy (ACE) [101] in the UK found that an affordable and manageable ten-year national energy conservation programme, directed at reducing space heating in buildings in all sectors would create 500,000 job-years of work - in other words the equivalent of employing 50,000 people for ten years (This study is included in Table 2). ERL estimated that 12 per cent of the jobs created would be in manufacturing, 65 per cent in installation and 23 per cent in technical and administrative support. The study did not estimate the number of jobs created in energy auditing and recording the current state of building stock. Roughly one third of the jobs were attributed to the multiplier and responding effects. The two sets of figures given for this study in Table 2 refer to a base case, which is considered to be well within industrial capability to deliver, and a maximum case [102].

In the US, where DSM has already received far more government and private sector attention, several recent studies have looked in detail at the jobs lost in particular energy supply sectors (displacement costs) in order to calculate the net employment impacts. These are summarised in Table 3. It is important to recognise that responding effects generated by the cost savings involved in DSM account for between 20 and 60 per cent of the total employment generated by DSM. The responding effects are highest (and most significant) where DSM replaces nuclear, which although relatively labour intensive, is a very expensive way of generating power. The levels of direct employment generated vary according to the labour intensity of the DSM programme conducted. For example, insulation measures tend to be more labour intensive than lighting efficiency initiatives.

Table 3: Net Job Generation by Demand Side Management (DSM) - Results of Various American Studies

Study	Job-years			
	Created in DSM	Created by respending	Displaced in conventional generation (1)	Net Gain (1)
British Columbia	6,357	9,144	3,641	11,860
Maine	4,212	2,770	1,883	5,099
Quebec	75,225	19,572	62,499	32,298
Washington State:				
Displacing nuclear	28,462	30,739	34,155	36,431
Displacing coal	28,462	42,124	15,939	43,262

*Source: Krier and Goodman, 1992.*Energy Efficiency: Opportunities for Employment. Prepared for Greenpeace UK by the Goodman Institute.
Note 1: Includes indirect employment.

55

"...pound for pound, investment in expenditure energy efficiency buys more direct jobs than investment in conventional energy supply options..."

These studies show that, pound for pound, investment in expenditure energy efficiency buys more direct jobs than investment in conventional energy supply options. However, because energy efficiency is more cost-effective in delivering each unit of energy than traditional supply options, the jobs lost in the latter industries may exceed those gained. But this is not the complete story. Because energy efficiency reduces energy bills, additional jobs can be created by the respending of that money. This, combined with multiplier effects, leads to net employment gains.

A recent study of energy investments by US electricity utilities found that efficiency measures could satisfy demand for electricity at a lower cost than traditional supply side options [103]. Using a national input-output model the study estimated that the additional employment generated by investment of $3.1 billion in DSM programmes (effectively providing almost 50 TWh [104]) in 1992 was over 75,000 jobs *(See Table*

Table 4: A Forecast of Jobs Generated by Demand Side Management Investments in Electricity Utilities in the United States

Gross employment generated in demand side management	82,460
Employment displaced in electricity generation	98,000
Employment generated by respending	91,010
Net employment gain	75,470

Source: Krier and Goodman, 1992. Energy Efficiency : Opportunities for Employment. *These figures are a forecast of the nationwide employment effects based on estimates of DSM investment.*

"...A £1.25 billion annual investment in insulation and energy efficiency in the homes of the fuel-poor could create 45,000 to 138,000 jobs..."

4). In the UK, Friends of the Earth has proposed a target for DSM investment of £1 billion per year *[105]*. Assuming a similar jobs-to-investment ratio, this would generate 36,000 jobs.

Friends of the Earth has also proposed a £1.25 billion annual investment in insulation and energy efficiency in the homes of the fuel-poor *[105]*. Applying the same ratio used above to this figure for investment suggests 45,000 jobs could be created from such an investment programme, while if the estimates from Table 1 are applied (£9,000-23,000 per job year), 54,000 to 138,000 jobs would be created. However, these latter estimates do not account for job losses in energy generation.

Generating jobs - renewable and efficient energy sources

Similarly, measures to improve the efficient supply of energy also have a positive impact on employment. For example, conventional power stations waste low-grade heat at a rate which exceeds the domestic sector's low-temperature heat demand. Combined Heat and Power (CHP) systems distribute this energy to households and offices in district heating schemes. CHP investments have been made in many cities throughout Europe and North America. As the technology associated with CHP advances, systems have been installed to serve dispersed suburbs as well as high-density areas. The economic benefits of CHP are in efficiency rather than the economies of scale associated with conventional power generation. Equally, job numbers are not reduced through centralisation because there are a larger number of smaller units. A recent survey of CHP schemes in the UK found that 83 per cent of CHP installations had an installed capacity of less than 1 MW *[106]*.

**"...Most conventional energy supply industries
are capital-intensive and create relatively few jobs..."**

It has been estimated that a 3,000MW CHP programme in the UK involving investments in nine major cities, including Sheffield, Newcastle, London, Leicester and Belfast, would create 140,000 person-years of employment over 10 to 15 years [107]. After accounting for the potential displacement of jobs in conventional generation, this implies that 7,875-12,535 additional jobs would be created over 10 to 15 years [108].

Even with a full-scale national energy efficiency programme, energy supply that relies on conventional fuels and technology would continue to have an enormous adverse environmental impact. In a sustainable economy, renewable energy sources will become increasingly important supply options. These too can have important employment as well as environmental benefits.

Most conventional energy supply industries are capital-intensive and create relatively few jobs. The oil and gas industry in Alberta, Canada, for instance, generates just 1.4 jobs for every $1 million worth of capital investment compared with 9.2 jobs in manufacturing, 13 in agriculture and 32 in service industries [109]. This is a continuing trend, as power stations have become larger in order to capture increased economies of scale and as fuel switching has favoured energy sources which require less labour (such as the shift from coal to gas).

The continuing focus by governments, industry and development banks on large capital-intensive energy generation capacity has negative employment impacts in developing countries too. In central and eastern Europe, the environmental, economic and social benefits of investing in demand side management are clear [110]. Yet the newly formed European Bank for Reconstruction and Development appears to have been most influenced by the current structure of the energy sector of its

"...replacing conventional energy sources with wind power could increase employment up to 396 per cent!"

main shareholder countries *[111]*. Only after consistent pressure from environmental groups has the Bank started to re-assess its approach to investing in demand side management *[112]*. Not only do these major investments generate fewer jobs than appropriate small scale renewable generation and energy efficiency, but they tie up capital which could be more productively invested. In Costa Rica and Brazil, for example, one quarter of their foreign debts are from borrowing for the construction of power plants and transmission lines *[110]*.

In the US, where diverse renewable sources of energy are most widely used, the employment impacts of these sustainable sources of energy have been shown to be positive *(see Table 5)*. In some of these cases, however, as the technologies and manufacturing processes are refined, the net jobs gain can be expected to decrease as economies of scale are achieved in manufacture and installation.

The UK wind resource is the most plentiful wind energy resource in Europe, and it is worthwhile examining this sector in some detail. A study by the American Wind Energy Association based on a comprehensive employment survey of wind plant operators and their service providers in California generated a figure of 460 jobs per TWh/ year for operation, maintenance and support *[113]*. This can be compared with estimates for direct employment in operation, service and maintenance by BTM Consult in Denmark of 230-440 jobs per TWh/ year *[113, 114]*. These figures suggest that replacing conventional energy sources with wind power could increase employment by 198-396 per cent!

The jobs arising from manufacturing wind power turbines can also be estimated, although comparative figures for conventional energy sources are not available. In Denmark, assuming a 20-25 year lifespan of each turbine, 88-146 further direct jobs would arise in manufacturing [115]. This gives a figure for total direct employment in wind of 528-586 which compares well with Flavin and Lenssen's preliminary estimate of 542 [109] (see Table 5).

Indirect employment was also calculated - in the Californian study this came to 1500 jobs per TWh/year. In Denmark indirect employment in the manufacturing process (eg component manufacture, tool manufacture) increased employment in manufacturing by around three times, to 12-15 person years per MW. This equates to a further 152-353 jobs per TWh.

Estimates of the job creation potential of on-shore wind-power for electricity generation in the UK can therefore be made using base figures from one of the Government's 'heightened environmental scenarios'[116]. In this scenario the contribution of wind power by 2005 ranges up to 30 TWh/year. This would produce some 6,900-13,800 jobs, or, assuming that coal power was replaced by wind power 3,420-10,320 additional jobs.

However, to reach this level of generation would require some 15,000-20,000MW of capacity to be installed over the next ten years. During this period the job gains could be higher assuming that UK manufacturing capacity was developed. To install capacity at this rate requires 6,600-8,800 direct jobs in turbine manufacturing, but including indirect jobs in manufacturing, the figure increases to 18,000-30,000 jobs [117].

According to the Government the maximum practicable resource for onshore wind-power in 2005 is 55 TWh/year [116, 118]. This, if realised, could create 6,270-18,920 additional direct jobs (if coal power were replaced by wind). The potential for manufacturing jobs would increase to 33,000-55,000 jobs of which 12,000-16,000 would be directly engaged in turbine manufacture.

"...In the case of off-shore wind-power, not only does the UK have the natural resources to develop, but also, it has arguably the best rough-sea engineering and operating skills in the world..."

However, the UK has, to a large extent, missed the boat for reaping substantial short- or medium-term benefits from the manufacture of on-shore wind-power technology, and although many components of Danish wind-turbines are manufactured in the UK [119] the overall gains in manufacturing sector would probably be less than these estimates suggest.

In the case of off-shore wind-power, however, the UK has an opportunity to gain an advantage. Not only does the UK have the natural resources to develop, but also, mainly due to the North Sea oil industry, it has arguably the best rough-sea engineering and operating skills in the world. In exploiting its off-shore potential for renewable power the UK could create employment and a potential export industry ahead of countries like Japan and the USA which usually beat Britain in exploiting

Table 5: Employment in Electricity Generation

Technology	Jobs generated (per TWh/year)
Nuclear	100
Geothermal	112
Coal (incl. mining)	116
Thermal Solar	248
Wind	440-460
Wind (including manufacturing)	542

*Sources: Flavin, C. and Lenssen, N. 1990.*Beyond the Petroleum Age.*Worldwatch; and Gipe, P. 1994. 'Overview of worldwide wind generation'. In*Renewable Energy: Climate change, energy and the environment. *Proceedings of the World Renewable Energy Congress. Pergamon Press.*

innovative new technologies. As the technology involved is so new, it is not yet possible to estimate the likely job-creation potential. However, a recent review by the Department of Trade and Industry (DTI) [116], while acknowledging the potential, assigned off-shore wind technology to the status of 'watching brief', undermining further research and development progress.

For active solar power, continuing research and development is recommended by the DTI *[116]*. It estimated that, by 2005, 7.7 TWh per year could be utilised in district heating schemes and for domestic hot water alone [116]. Using the figures presented by Flavin and Lennson *[109] (see Table 5)* it can be estimated that active solar would involve around 1,900 jobs, and if this capacity replaced coal fired generation there would be a net employment gain of just over 1,000 jobs.

In the energy industry, as in motor manufacturing, at least some skills are transferable. For example, petroleum geologists and oil-well crews have the type of skills needed in the geothermal power industry; and, as indicated above, sea-engineering skills will be needed in development of off-shore wind-power. Moreover, jobs in the renewable energy sector are generally clean and safe - employees would not be required to clean up oil spills or decommission 'hot' nuclear plants.

The location of many renewable energy supply stations also has implications for employment. In developed countries wind farms can bring about direct and indirect employment benefits in rural areas which are often not touched by government schemes to increase employment. In many developing countries, simple and locally-based renewable technologies can provide a cheap and reliable source of energy in more rural areas which can help create jobs *[120]*.

"...wind farms can bring about direct and indirect employment benefits in rural areas which are often not touched by government schemes to increase employment..."

Conclusion

The opportunities for employment creation through feasible and economic sustainable energy generation and use in the UK are substantial. Estimates suggest that up to 81,000 additional direct and indirect jobs could be created by energy efficiency investments which would also improve the housing conditions of the fuel-poor. Economic efficiency investments by Government and householders can be combined with increased fuel prices (a carbon tax is discussed below in the section on tax reform).

Moreover, further jobs could be created through the expansion of renewable energy sources at the expense of nuclear and coal-fired power. Estimates suggest that the UK has the potential to create up to 10,300 additional jobs in utilising on-shore wind resources, and 1,000 additional jobs in utilising solar energy, by 2005.

Resource Use

The world has a limited amount of natural resources and a limited capacity to assimilate the wastes produced by the consumption of resources. In order to progress toward environmental sustainability, economic activities must become far more efficient in using resources and materials. Efficiency gains can be made in refining raw materials and the use of commodity materials in manufacturing. Pollution control regulation, considered above, is one policy tool which can help stimulate the essential changes; fiscal penalties, considered later, are another.

Product design can reflect the waste management hierarchy of 'reduce, re-use, recycle, energy recovery'. Products can be designed to use less materials but retain the same performance. A recent Dutch survey found that a material saving of ten to 30 per cent can be made across a range of domestic and commercial goods [121]. Products can be designed for durability [122] and with repair and re-use in mind. Products can be designed for disassembly so that used materials can be recycled as source materials for other products. Finally, when recycling is no longer feasible, energy can be recovered from the materials before the residual waste is disposed of in a managed way.

As such advances are made, jobs can be created. And although there will be job losses in industries and areas which produce virgin materials, the evidence available indicates that these will be overshadowed by the employment benefits accompanying improved resource use.

"...a shift to a completely returnable system for beer and carbonated soft drinks would lead to a net increase of between 3,200 and 4,000 jobs in the United Kingdom..."

Maintaining jobs - repair and reuse

Product repair and re-use have employment benefits. Repairing and reconditioning products are, in general, labour-intensive activities, in comparison with disposal and new manufacture. The packaging industry provides prime examples of products which are designed to be thrown away and at the same time waste resources. Friends of the Earth research highlights how trends in the industry continue to waste valuable resources [123]. One example is the trend away from re-usable drinks containers. In 1977, 60 per cent of both packaged carbonated soft drinks and packaged beer was sold in returnable containers; but by 1987 the figures had dropped to 19 and 23.3 per cent respectively [124]. Other studies have shown that not only would resource use efficiency be improved if refillable containers were used, but more jobs would be created. A report for the European Commission on the employment impacts of glass re-use and recycling concluded that: *"The use of returnable systems generates more employment than non-returnable beverage container systems"* [125].

The report estimated that a shift to a completely returnable system for beer and carbonated soft drinks would lead to a net increase of between 3,200 and 4,000 jobs in the United Kingdom over three years. Supermarkets confirm that additional staff would be needed to deal with returnable containers [126].

Extending the lifespan of durable products can also increase labour needs. For example, reconditioning a car with a ten-year life-span, to make it last another ten years leads to an energy saving of 42 per cent. Additionally, 56 per cent more labour-time is required in comparison with the manufacture of a new car [127]. It should be noted that such products need to be designed to allow up-grading in accordance with

**"...many of the 26,000 jobs in the industry
are reliant upon recycling. .."**

tighter environmental standards as they are introduced. Research on this concept of up-grading is being promoted as part of a UK research programme *[128]*.

Throwing away jobs

Recycling is already an important source of jobs, although no Government statistics are compiled and comparatively little research has been carried out on the subject. Some materials sectors, such as metals, have established recycling industries and others, such as plastics, are comparatively new. In the UK paper industry, recycled pulp accounts for 55-60 per cent of the industry's main raw material with 34 per cent of the virgin pulp being imported *[129, 130]*. Clearly, many of the 26,000 jobs in the industry are reliant upon recycling. Although only 30 per cent of UK waste paper is recovered *[131]*, it is estimated that a further 3,000 jobs already exist in the collection and processing of waste paper [132]. Increasing the collection rate to 75 per cent, the level achieved in the Netherlands, may therefore create a further 4,500 jobs, but at the cost of some jobs in forestry in the UK and abroad.

Recycling product components is also recognised to be a growth area which will create jobs. The development of cars which can be dismantled to separate re-usable components and materials has been forecast to result in a net growth in employment *[30]*.

A research report for the European Commission examining the employment impacts of alternative waste-management strategies found that considerable employment gains could be made by increasing recycling and energy recovery from a number of waste streams *[133]*. In

**"...landfill is the worst option
and materials separation for recycling
the best option in terms of increasing employment..."**

particular, the report noted that the greater the degree of treatment and processing, the greater the job intensity. In the case of solvent waste, landfilling provided just 1.6 jobs per 1,000 tonnes per year, incineration 2.7, and recovery and processing for substitution 3.73. For waste oil the estimates of jobs provided per 1,000 tonnes per year were 0.01 for disposal to sewer, 0.63 for burning on-site, 2.24 for collection and landfill, 2.75 for collection and refining as a substitute oil and 4.87 for collection, refining and blending as a substitute for virgin lubricants.

In England some 335,000 of the annual total of 380,000 tonnes of waste oil is already recycled. Applying the figures above suggests that 900 to 1,600 jobs have been created in comparison with disposing of the waste oil to sewer. On the other hand only 15 per cent of solvent wastes are recovered and treated. According to DTI estimates over 2.5 million tonnes of 'special wastes' are dumped, and 'almost all' of this is solvent waste [134]. Assuming that solvents comprise 75 per cent of special wastes, recovery rather than landfilling of this waste could create almost 4,000 additional jobs.

In the case of municipal waste, both the European Commission report [133] and research carried out in the United States (see Table 6), conclude that landfill is the worst option and materials separation for recycling the best option in terms of increasing employment. In New York, recycling generated between 400 and almost 600 jobs per million tonnes processed, while landfilling generated less than 50. In Vermont, where economies of scale are less - and probably more comparable with the UK - recycling generated 550 to 2,000 jobs per million tonnes, compared with 50 to 360 for landfill [135].

If the New York and Vermont figures are applied to the UK's 20 million

**"...A more ambitious, but practical,
target for 2000 - 40 per cent recycling - would create 2,450
to 11,550 additional jobs..."**

tonne domestic waste stream, achieving the Government's target of recycling 25 per cent of our rubbish would create 1,400 to 6,600 additional jobs by 2000. A more ambitious, but practical, target for 2000 - 40 per cent recycling - would create 2,450 to 11,550 additional jobs. Moreover, domestic waste accounts for only a small proportion of the total recyclable waste produced in the UK, so the overall job creation potential of recycling is likely to be substantially greater than these figures indicate.

The separation and composting of organic waste was also identified as having job creation potential by the US and European studies. According to Government figures approximately 70 per cent of the domestic waste

Table 6: Jobs per 1 Million Tons of Waste Processed, New York City

Types of Waste Disposal	Number of Jobs
Landfills	40 - 60
Incenerators	100 - 290
Mixed Solid Waste Composting	200 - 300
Recycling Facilities	400 - 590

Source: New York City, Department of Sanitation. Cited in Renner, M. 1991. Jobs in a sustainable economy. *Worldwatch Paper 104. Washington DC, Worldwatch Institute.*

**"...In the US, several states provide grants
or low interest loans for businesses developing
products from recycled materials..."**

stream may be either recyclable or compostable [136], so employment gains may again be higher.

Regional economic development studies have explored the potential benefits of recycling. The Scottish Development Agency estimated that materials recycling in Scotland could create 1,000 new jobs and save up to £34 million of materials each year [137]. In West Yorkshire a new forum has brought together five local authorities, four universities and industry to encourage economic development through establishing recycling businesses [138].

An alternative estimate can be derived from turnover forecasts made by the DTI. At a national level the DTI estimates that of the 87,000 jobs in the waste management industry some ten to 20 per cent (8,700 to 17,400) are concerned with recycling [139]. Moreover, the DTI forecasts an increase in turnover in the waste management industry from £3 billion in 1992 to £5 billion by 1997-98 [139]. Even if recycling turnover increases only at the same rate as the rest of the industry, this would imply the creation of up to 11,500 additional jobs in recycling, although even 25 per cent recycling of domestic waste is not expected on this timescale. Even this estimate may be on the low side, as recycling is rapidly expanding, and is more labour intensive than other waste management techniques. The DTI supports the view that recycling should be supported as an industrial sector in the same way that other sectors receive Government support [134]. In the US, several states provide grants or low interest loans for business development of new markets for products and new industrial start-ups that will manufacture products from recycled materials [140].

Conclusion

If sustainable development is to be achieved, the potential for improving resource efficiency to reduce environmental damage and create jobs must be realised. Governments need to provide the regulatory and other incentives which guide industry towards the task of innovating and operating according to the principles of resource efficiency and waste minimisation. Together governments, industry and research bodies need to do far more to find new solutions to make resource use sustainable.

The current profligate consumption of resources denies the opportunity for greater employment. The potential for job creation exists throughout the waste hierarchy. Estimates suggest that: returnable beer and soft-drinks bottles could increase UK employment by up to 4,000; if waste paper collection were to be raised to levels achieved in the Netherlands, 4,500 jobs could be created; over 4,000 jobs could be created through the recycling of waste oils and solvents; and recycling 40 per cent of domestic waste instead of landfilling it could create up to 11,500 additional jobs. Policy change to increase the costs of waste disposal and to enhance markets for recycled materials would help release this potential.

Agriculture

Agriculture is an indispensable part of the management of the natural environment. It is one of the fundamental sectors of any economy and the lifeblood of rural economies throughout the world. Yet, increasingly, the development path followed by agriculture over the last few decades is being questioned on economic, environmental and social grounds. As agricultural production has increased, the price paid by the natural environment and wild species has also increased, while the economic benefits have accrued mostly to a small minority.

Since the end of the Second World War, agricultural policies in most developed countries have sought to increase output per hectare. This has led to larger farm units, intensive farm production systems, increased mechanisation and an increase in external inputs, such as pesticides and artificial fertilizers. As a consequence, employment in farming has plummeted. Between 1945 and 1992, the number of regular full-time and part-time hired and family workers on English farms fell from 478,000 to 135,000 according to MAFF census figures [141]. The National Economic Development Council has forecast that in the 1990s a further 17 to 26 per cent of farm labour will be shed [142]. In the US the size of the agricultural work force fell from about 17 per cent, or ten million workers, to about two per cent, or 2.5 million workers from 1947 to 1985 [143]. In fact, the labour used to farm an acre in the US has declined by 75 per cent while farm output has doubled [143].

In addition, the economic benefits of increased production have tended to bypass many rural economies as the processing of agricultural produce and food production has become increasingly centralised in order to gain economies of scale. As a result, further jobs have been lost in rural communities as rural services, such as schools, shops, doctors and public transport have steadily declined.

The costs to the environment of intensifying agriculture have been alarming. Since 1945 the UK has lost 95 per cent of its wildflower-rich meadows, 30 to 50 per cent of ancient lowland woodlands, 50 to 60 per cent of lowland heathland, 140,000 miles of hedgerows and over 50 per cent of lowland fens, valley and basin mires [144]. According to the UK's statutory nature conservation agency, the predominant causes of these losses have been changes in agricultural practice. In addition the contamination of rivers, groundwater and drinking water from the use of artificial nitrate fertilizers and pesticides has become an issue of national and international concern [145, 146]. A significant proportion of the multi-million pound costs incurred in water treatment could be saved if more sustainable practices reduced emissions from this source.

As a result many farmers are turning to farming practices that reduce the need for agrochemical inputs and cut the potential for environmental damage through efficient use of natural and biological resources. Such reduced dependence on external inputs represents progress toward sustainable development. Farming practices such as low-input and organic farming are collectively referred to in general terms as sustainable agriculture [141]. They include a range of technological and management options, such as integrated pest management which rely on a fuller understanding of biological and ecological interactions and nutrient cycles.

"...Sustainable farming practices typically require both more skilled and unskilled labour than conventional farming..."

Growing employment

There is already evidence that farmers practicing sustainable agriculture often produce high per hectare yields with significant reductions in costs per unit of crop harvested and also employ more people [143]. Such farming practices typically require both more skilled and unskilled labour than conventional farming [143]. For example, patch spraying can reduce farmers' herbicide bills by 95 per cent with no impact on yields by effectively substituting labour and knowledge for excessive pesticide use [147].

A recent study of the development of organic farming in Britain concluded that employment gains went beyond the farms concerned and extended to processing industries [148]. A considerably higher proportion of output from organic farms is processed locally, bringing benefits in the total number of jobs created and for local rural economies suffering high levels of unemployment:

"... the direct impact on the rural economy in terms of farm employment offers advantages over conventional farming, and (that) any possible disadvantages in terms of reduced inputs may be more than offset by increased processing" [148].

Very few studies have begun to quantify job gains, as the principal focus of research has been on the profitability of the new practices. However, recently published studies of the economics of organic farming in Germany and Denmark offer some preliminary data [149]. In Germany, in 1991/2, 19 per cent more labour was used on organic farms per 100 hectares than on comparable conventional farms [150]. However, the research suggests that the labour difference may decline in the longer

"...if just one quarter of UK farming was converted to organic production, employment in agriculture would increase by 30,000-45,000 jobs..."

term to only 10 per cent. In Denmark in 1988, 75 per cent more labour was used, although some of this may be accounted for by structural differences and a figure of 30 per cent is suggested as more representative [151].

Using the central range of these figures (20-30 per cent) suggests that if just one quarter of UK farming was converted to organic production, employment in agriculture would increase by 30,000-45,000 jobs [152]. This could only be achieved by active policy change to support organic agriculture. In the shorter term a target of 10 per cent organic within ten to 15 years may be feasible, given experience in Germany and Sweden. This could generate 12,000-18,000 additional jobs. However, the current Ministry of Agriculture, Fisheries and Food (MAFF) target for England is just to triple the area of organic production, to around 75,000 hectares over 5 years [153].

Lower per hectare yields in organic farming mean that more land would be required to produce the same quantity of food, and this may mean that even after surpluses were eradicated, land otherwise being set aside as a result of European Union policy would be brought back into production. The set-aside policy followed by the Government has in fact resulted in the loss of one full-time job for every 130 hectares of land set-aside [154] - a total of 3,791 jobs lost so far [155].

> **"...if 440,000 to 590,000 hectares of
> broadleaved woodland were planted and managed
> for timber production, then some 3,300-4,400
> jobs could be created..."**

Out of the woods

Other more sustainable farm management practices have also been identified as generating jobs. One example is farmers managing existing semi-natural woodlands rather than establishing monoculture conifer plantations. Input-output simulation studies for farms in Wales forecast that introducing conifer plantations would create only 50 extra jobs over the next 40 years compared to 150 extra jobs through the management of 20,000 hectares of semi-natural woodland - which would also generate twice as much income for landowners [148, 156]. As with organic farming, it is suggested that increasing hardwood supplies, in small amounts of gradually improving quality, could stimulate the creation of new jobs in processing and marketing activity. Extrapolating from these figures, if 440,000 to 590,000 hectares of broadleaved woodland were planted and managed for timber production (the area needed to substitute for the UK's tropical hardwood imports [157]), then some 3,300-4,400 jobs could be created.

Conclusion

Despite the positive evidence that has been gathered to date, research has yet to fully embrace the study of the economic impacts of sustainable agriculture. In particular the Government has failed to investigate an alternative policy approach to reap the benefits from a shift toward ecologically and socially sustainable farming practices.

It is now critical that the Government funds trial programmes and research which investigates more fully the potential for sustainable agriculture to bring environmental, social and economic benefits, following the example of the Boxworth research project on reducing chemical inputs [158]. In particular the wider employment benefits for rural communities need to be examined.

Sustainable agricultural practices are more labour intensive than conventional ones. Moreover local processing of the output of farms, brings benefits for local rural economies suffering high levels of unemployment. Enhanced financial support for conversion to organic agriculture and reformed agricultural support payments could pay dividends in terms of jobs.

A feasible target of ten per cent of production converted to organic agriculture within ten to 15 years is estimated to generate 12,000-18,000 additional jobs. In the longer term, increasing the area of lowland broadleaved woodland to begin to substitute for the UK's tropical hardwood imports could create up to 4,400 jobs over 40 years.

Making the change

"...governments and institutions remain largely wedded to the false premise that economic growth is needed in order to provide the resources for environmental protection..."

From these sector studies it is clear that substantial opportunities exist for combining job creation, environmental protection and wise resource use through sustainable development. Equally it is clear that governments and industry are failing to realise these opportunities. A business-as-usual approach will continue to generate further problems for employment and the environment. In order to change, ambitious but practicable policy initiatives are needed from government and the private sector. In many cases such initiatives will be closely interlinked. As a recent paper for the European Commission emphasises, employment and environmental challenges may both:

"even be symptoms of the same defect in our present pattern of economic development: an inefficient use of resources, represented by under-use of human resources and over-use of environmental resources ... the only viable and lasting solution may be a strategy that addresses both concerns at the same time" [6].

Four important themes in delivering sustainable development highlight this commonality: policy integration, public investment policies, training provision and tax reform.

"...the failure to fully take on board employment considerations in the formation of environmental policies may not only exacerbate job losses, but also spur resistance to change and handicap efforts to improve environmental protection..."

Policy integration

As the quote from the Brundtland Report at the beginning of this paper makes clear, sustainable development cannot be achieved simply through improved environmental protection. As Agenda 21, the global action plan for the 21st Century agreed at the Earth Summit in 1992, states:

"The overall objective is to improve or restructure the decision-making process so that consideration of socio-economic and environmental issues is fully integrated" [159].

It is also true that the failure to fully take on board employment considerations in the formation of environmental policies may not only exacerbate job losses, but also spur resistance to change and handicap efforts to improve environmental protection.

Despite this, governments and institutions remain largely wedded to the false premise that economic growth is needed in order to provide the resources for environmental protection [160]. For example the European Commission recently delayed the publication of its proposed amendments to the Environmental Impact Assessment Directive, reportedly due to a general "jobs before the environment" atmosphere [161]. Environmental damage continues, and new environmental risks arise, but only marginal remedial measures are introduced. If employment levels are to increase at the same time as the environment is protected and natural resources conserved, then this dislocation must be tackled. It is particularly important in those policy areas where future needs are addressed, such as research and development, training and infrastructure investment.

The need for pollution control laws to be formulated in order to stimulate innovation and the development of clean technologies was noted earlier. Enforcement of such regulations is equally important. A representative of the Allied Engineering and Electrical Union points to the UK's coal industry as an example where failure to implement environmental measures has led to the loss of jobs:

"The government's decision to scale down its flue gas desulphurisation programme has meant an increase in imported low sulphur coal. This has profound implications in terms of job losses in the coal industry, a damaging effect on our balance of payments and lost opportunities in manufacturing new equipment" [162].

Yet regulation works best when supported by other policies. In the case of coal-fired power stations, in 1993 the director of Her Majesty's Inspectorate of Pollution (HMIP) urged the Government to fund a demonstration plant using 'clean coal technology' as a means of encouraging the development of cleaner combustion technology [163]. The Government refused [163].

Perhaps the most important step in policy integration in any market-based economy is to consider environmental costs fully in decision-making. Existing national accounting methods do not put an economic value on environmental damage created by economic activity or on economic services provided by the environment. Such accounts tend systematically to bias economic analysis of environmental policies by overestimating the welfare gains of a growth in gross domestic product.

One example of bias caused by the failure to cost the environmental impact of different development paths is the comparison between road and rail transport. Car drivers and lorries are heavily subsidized in most

Table 7: External Costs of Passenger Transport (Germany, 1993)

| Category | Cost ($US per thousand passenger km) | | |
	Rail	Air	Car
Air pollution	1.05	8.54	17.08
Carbon dioxide	2.57	10.76	5.26
Noise	0.35	1.87	1.40
Accidents	1.64	0.23	16.03
Total	5.50	21.41	39.78

Source: Kageson, P. 1993. Getting the prices right: A European scheme for making transport pay its true costs. *Stockholm: European Federation for Transport and Environment.*

developed countries. A number of recent studies have separated 'internal' costs - those which the driver pays - from 'external' costs - those borne by others or society as a whole [98].

Several attempts to quantify these external costs have been made. For example, in one of the more conservative estimates, David Pearce, former adviser to the Department of the Environment, estimated that the external costs of road transport, not including road costs, are as high as £25.7 billion, compared with road-tax revenues of £14.7 billion [164]. Because this issue has not been addressed for so long, the calculations for these external costs are still developing. In another study, the costs of air

"..a more coordinated approach to taxation, commonly referred to as 'ecological tax reform' could produce additional employment benefits for the economy as a whole..."

pollution, noise and accidents were shown to be far higher for car travel than for train *(see Table 7)*. As long as such costs are ignored, policy convergence will not occur and decision-making will be prejudiced against sustainable development.

Tax Reform

In each of the sectors considered, a range of policies and specific measures are required to maximise the net gain in employment. In some sectors, such as energy, considerable attention has been given to the use of taxation as a means to drive the changes that can bring about economic and environmental benefits. As Friends of the Earth has shown in the case of energy, taxation is one of a range of policy measures that should be used in a coordinated way [165]. In this case, taxation to increase the cost of energy is one incentive to increasing efficiency of energy use.

Similar roles for taxation can be suggested for other environmental problems such as waste disposal [166]. However, there may be problems in the implementation of such taxes. While the overall effect of the environmental policy change may be beneficial, in a transitional period taxes could increase costs to the extent that job-losses in polluting industries will result. Because these industries are concentrated in particular regions, any impacts of unemployment would be similarly concentrated [167].

However, a more coordinated approach to taxation, commonly referred to as 'ecological tax reform' could produce additional employment benefits for the economy as a whole.

83

"...an increased escalatory tax on road fuel of 17.6 per cent per annum from 1996 could increase employment by 1.275 million by the year 2005..."

The main thrust of ecological tax reform is that the burden of taxation should be shifted from taxing labour to taxing environmentally-damaging activities such as waste production, excessive energy use and traffic congestion. Increased taxes on environmentally-damaging activities would be compensated for by reductions in other taxes, such as those on labour. In other words, governments should tax environmental 'bads' instead of economic 'goods'. The price of labour compared with energy and waste disposal would decrease, with beneficial consequences for the level of employment in the economy, importantly without stimulating inflation.

The share of taxes and charges placed on labour costs in European Union member states has continuously increased over the past two decades and now accounts for almost 50 per cent of the overall tax burden [6]. In contrast, the price of energy and natural resources in real terms has fallen over the last two decades, with only ten per cent of the tax burden falling on the use of natural resources [6].

The relative price change would encourage companies to make productivity gains by cutting inputs of energy and raw materials and outputs of pollution, rather than through reducing labour costs. Positive employment effects are also likely because the sectors likely to experience increased demand as a result of this relative price shift, such as telecommunications and financial services [168], are not only less energy intensive but also more labour intensive.

The highest estimates of increased employment from such reform come from a recent study which considered the likely effects in the UK of an increased escalatory tax on road fuel of 17.6 per cent per annum from 1996. The study suggests that with the revenue being recycled through

"...The greatest employment gains are achieved by recycling the revenue as reductions in employers' National Insurance contributions..."

a decrease in employers' national insurance contributions, this could increase employment by 1.275 million by the year 2005 [169]. This would leave the base-level of unemployment at 1.6 million - the same as in the mid-1980s credit boom. The increase in fuel efficiency and reduction in car use resulting from the tax would save 21.2 million tonnes of carbon emissions (a reduction equivalent to that achievable by a carbon/energy tax increasing to $10 per barrel by 2000). Another study in Germany and the UK broadly corroborated these findings: even with a projected two per cent growth rate in the economy, carbon dioxide emissions could fall by 3.45 per cent per annum and employment rise by 4.6 per cent per annum [169].

Studies carried out at Cambridge University demonstrate that a more general tax on the carbon content of fuels will bring net employment gains [169, 170, 171]. The greatest employment gains are achieved by recycling the revenue as reductions in employers' National Insurance contributions. However, these jobs (278,000 by the year 2005) are significantly less than the potential gains from the tax on road-fuel described above [169]. More jobs may be created by directing the reductions in National Insurance contributions to low-skilled, lower-paid jobs [172].

The European Commission is now actively pursuing the idea of ecological tax reform. As part of its justification the Commission produced an analysis of the economic impacts of a carbon tax increasing to $10 dollars per barrel, particularly the effects of reducing employers' social security contributions by using the receipts of the tax. The findings of one analysis are summarised in Table 8. This indicates that for no net cost to the public account, and an increase in consumer prices of less than one per cent, some 650,000 jobs would be created in the UK, Denmark,

"...Over 200,000 of the new jobs would be in the manufacturing sector..."

Ireland, Belgium, Luxembourg and The Netherlands. Over 200,000 of the new jobs would be in the manufacturing sector. As Table 8 shows, some sectors, such as power generation, would suffer a small loss of jobs. Another analysis of the European Commission's proposals produced similar overall results. Of the 697,000 jobs created in the six countries studied, 150,000 would be in the UK. The sectors benefiting most would be industry, gaining 69,000 jobs and services, gaining 43,000 [173]. Such tax reform could be undertaken unilaterally by a single nation and benefits would still arise [174].

Table 8: Economic Implications of EU Tax Reform

Macro-economic indicator	Change (per cent)
GDP	+0.13
Investment	- 0.02
Private consumption	+0.14
Consumer prices	+0.97
Public account	0.00
	Jobs (thousands)
Employment	+650.32
- energy	-1.61
- manufacturing	+218.56

Source: Europe Environment No 421, 30-11-1993.

**"...such investments are likely to stimulate innovation
and bring balance of trade benefits..."**

Moreover, ecological tax reform can deliver administrative objectives as well as environmental and economic ones. For example, one of the arguments put forward to support ecological tax reform is that it can be a more efficient way (in administrative terms) of collecting tax than conventional means [175].

It is also possible to construct environmental taxes in such a way as to provide a continued incentive for companies and consumers to reduce their use of environmental resources. However, at the political level increasing revenue dependence on ecological 'bads' could discourage governments from implementing other policies to reduce the consumption of environmental resources. Fortunately, the benefits noted above can be obtained from relatively marginal reforms involving just one to five per cent of tax revenue [172].

Public investment

Laying a foundation for sustainable development needs investment in appropriate infrastructure and human development. The use of public investment as means of stimulating employment and the economy is not new and is endorsed by the European Commission's recent White Paper on Growth, Competitiveness and Employment[81]. However the specific proposals supported by this White Paper include conventional infrastructure investments which are both environmentally damaging and inefficient at creating employment, such as major roads.

Public investment expenditures often entail measures with high direct and indirect employment effects. In the sector studies presented above several examples of infrastructure programmes which could both protect

"...the cost to the UK economy of keeping one person unemployed for a year is over £9,000..."

the environment and create jobs have been outlined. Moreover, such investments are likely to stimulate innovation and bring balance of trade benefits. These include investments in public transport, energy demand management, collection and treatment of waste water, collection and separation of municipal waste and the provision of materials recycling infrastructure.

Job Creation

Evidence gathered by the International Labour Organisation (ILO) from Sweden, France and Germany shows that employment creation schemes and environmental protection programmes can be successfully combined [176]. Such effective environmental job creation schemes also greatly reduce the costs incurred by the government and tax payers in social security payments and lost tax revenue.

Given continued high levels of unemployment, and government expenditure on schemes designed solely or partly to create jobs, it is worth briefly examining the costs and benefits of jobs created by environmental policy.

At present the cost to the UK economy of keeping one person unemployed for a year is over £9,000 [177]. This must be deducted from the costs of job creation (examples of which were shown in *Table 1*) if the net cost to the taxpayer is to be established. Desirable environmental investments in public transport and energy efficiency are therefore effectively cheaper than the figures in *Table 1* suggest. It seems likely that accounting for this saving would make such investments more economically viable, and indeed, in some cases such job creation would save public money!

Environmental job creation schemes can create employment, develop employees' skills and protect the environment at the same time, in a variety of ways. Examples include building insulation schemes, cycle-path construction and nature conservation projects. Many of these programmes are likely to be labour-intensive and therefore provide good direct job-creation potential. However, more capital intensive environmental investments, such as water treatment - although more expensive per worker directly employed - can indirectly create more jobs.

Training provision

In order to make the change to sustainable development as efficient and beneficial as possible for the environment, employment and the economy, governments and the private sector need to stimulate and provide relevant training. Although small-scale schemes have been set-up in the UK, there is no comprehensive and properly resourced national environmental training programme.

The inadequacies of training have already presented problems in the implementation of environmental policies. A report by the Royal Commission on Environmental Pollution examining waste management and, in particular, the 'duty of care' for waste, criticised the industry for a lack of professionalism and training [178]. In a report for the Department of the Environment, the consultancy ECOTEC noted that the 'duty of care' provisions in the Environmental Protection Act 1990 required a *"very significant increase in the level of training provision"* [179].

The likely disjuncture between sectors and regions where job losses and gains occur reinforces the arguments for investment in training and

**"...the private sector must recognise that
the 'business as usual' approach lies at the heart
of global environmental and employment problems..."**

re-training. The International Labour Office (ILO) identified six priority sectors for training - environmental management in the public sector, water management, industrial pollution control, amenity development, environmental control in agriculture and solid waste management *[31]*.

Directing the Private Sector

One theme which has run through this paper is the key role which the private sector has to play in achieving sustainable development. Companies have made and continue to make many decisions which cause environmental degradation and many which result in substantial job losses in particular regions. These same companies also have the potential to innovate and manage their operations in a manner which is compatible with sustainable development. Indeed, if sustainable development is to become a reality this potential has to be realised.

The influence of the corporate world is increasing in environmental matters *[30]*. Despite this trend, or possibly because of it, the responsibilities of the private sector in achieving sustainable development have not been adequately addressed in international forums, most importantly at the Earth Summit in 1992. In contrast, governments, recognising the power of the private sector, are keen to increase its involvement in policy-making initiatives which cover the environment, such as the European Commission's Fifth Environmental Action Programme.

However, in order to assist in developing policies which will bring sustainable development, the private sector must recognise that the 'business as usual' approach lies at the heart of global environmental and employment problems. As the economist Ray Mishan says, with regard to the claim that environmental problems are best dealt with by an extension of property rights and competitive markets:

"after examining the habitual pattern of economic logic common to pro-market economists, and after ruminating on some of the environmental facts of life, we have had to conclude that such a claim cannot be vindicated" [180].

Yet the main representative bodies of the private sector, such as the International Chamber of Commerce, appear intent on protecting business as usual. Governments must act to direct the drive and strength of the private sector towards environmental sustainability goals. The alternative, where much of the private sector continues to exploit the rhetoric of sustainable development to further its own short-term and unsustainable objectives, cannot be an option.

Summary
and Conclusions

"...It is bad environmental management, not environmental regulation, which poses a greater threat to jobs in industry.... Strong environmental protection laws are not associated with reduced competitiveness in the global economy..."

That environmentally sustainable development offers the only hope for sufficient employment in the long-term is generally accepted by both decision-makers and the public. This paper has presented evidence from a range of economic sectors demonstrating that significant opportunities for society to realise environmental and net employment gains also exist in the short- and medium-term.

This paper has directly addressed some of the myths traditionally surrounding the relationship between jobs and environmental protection. None of them can be justified. It is bad environmental management, not environmental regulation, which poses a greater threat to jobs in industry. The car, so long the motor for economic growth, no longer holds the key to future development paths, despite its dominant position in most developed country economies. Strong environmental protection laws are not associated with reduced competitiveness in the global economy - in fact those countries which enact and enforce tough regulation have also generated the most dynamic and successful economies.

The need to integrate economic and environmental decision making - a key tenet of sustainable development - has been highlighted in this paper. The argument that economic growth must come first in order to afford environmental protection is an anachronism that policy makers must comprehensively reject as they confront the very real challenges of deteriorating environments and unacceptably high levels of unemployment. Yet the powerful interests ranged in defence of the

**"...the UK economy could gain 33,000
to 78,000 additional jobs directly through
environmental policy. If indirect job creation
is included, over 700,000 jobs may be
created by 2005..."**

economic status quo continue to drive a wedge between economic and environmental objectives. The private sector and government (at all levels) must adopt policies which have the vision and strength to reap the double benefit of environmental protection and employment gains. The policies needed are likely to lift economic development out of its current unsustainable rut onto a sustainable path and will also make the transition as smooth and efficient as possible.

This paper has exposed the lack of extensive quantified research and best practice demonstrations in most economic sectors on the employment benefits of environmental conservation and sustainable resource-use policies. Yet the existing evidence suggests there are substantial job gains to be made.

There is evidence that environmental policy has already led to an increase in employment - estimated at between 8,700-17,400 in the recycling industry and over 100,000 in pollution control in the UK, and many more worldwide. While there may be other more efficient ways of creating jobs, the job-creation effect is merely a secondary benefit of the environmental policy. Moreover, the available evidence suggests that current environmental policy has resulted in far fewer jobs lost than those created.

In the future, highly conservative estimates, summarised in Table9, based on empirical and modelled studies suggest that the UK economy could gain in the order of 33,000 to 78,000 additional jobs directly through environmental policy by 2005 [181]. Economic and econometric modelling suggests that substantially greater increases may arise from indirect job creation, through respending effects, for example, resulting in a total gain of over 700,000 by 2005 [182]. This would save money

Table 9: Selected estimates by sector

Measure	Jobs created	Notes
Direct only		
Wind (on-shore)	3,420-18,920	2005
Solar (active)	1,000	2005
CHP	7,875-12,535	10-15 yrs
Recycling (domestic)	2,450-11,550	2000
Public transport	6,475-15,740	1995
Organic farming	12-18,000	10-15 yrs

All these estimates are of additional jobs. Other assumptions are explained in the text.

Indirect included		
Wind (on-shore)	37,400-107,800	2005 *
Polluter Pays Principle	200,000	2005
Investment in water quality	696,000	2005
Energy efficiency/DSM	50,000-81,000	2005

* does not fully account for compensatory losses in manufacturing.

Tax revenue recycled		
Carbon tax	278,000	2005
Road fuel tax	1,275,000	2005

"...In this scenario the savings from reduced unemployment would be even greater, exceeding £4.5 billion..."

from the public purse. Each person-year of unemployment in the UK costs £9,000. If half of the new jobs were taken by currently unemployed people [183] then the saving to the UK exchequer would be over £3.15 billion every year.

Moreover, if the policy measures used were reinforced by tax reform, recycling revenue into reduced employers' national insurance payments, the total jobs gain may be far greater, easily exceeding a million, according to one estimate. In this scenario the savings from reduced unemployment would be even greater, exceeding £4.5 billion.

Although these are only estimates, based in some cases on relatively crude assumptions, the scale of the projected employment benefits emphasises how important it is that the issue is addressed with more vigour by Government and the private sector.

Friends of the Earth, for its part, intends to use this overview paper as the starting point for more detailed research in particular sectors. But it is government and the private sector who should be primarily resourcing such work. If this does not occur in the UK, we will continue to miss out on employment opportunities while degrading and despoiling the natural environment we all depend upon.

Notes and references

1.   Report of the Task Force on the Environment, "Our Children's World. Steelworkers and the Environment", in United Steelworkers of America, *Report of the Committee on Future Directions of the Union*, 25th Constitutional Convention, Toronto, Canada, August 27-31, 1990.

2.   Organisation for Economic Cooperation and Development, 1984.*The Impact of Environmental Policy on Employment.* Background paper for the OECD Conference on Environment and Economics, Paris.

3.   World Commission on Environment and Development, 1987.*Our Common Future.* Oxford: University Press.

4.   Quoted in *Economist,* July 9th 1994. "Help Wanted", p.27.

5.   *Financial Times,* April 18th 1994. "IMF predicts world growth of 3% in 1994".

6.   European Commission, 1993. *Economic Growth, Employment and Environmental Sustainability: a strategic view for the Community.* Working paper of the Informal Environment Council.

7.   United States, Japan, Germany, France, United Kingdom, Italy and Canada.

8.   *The Economist,* March 12th 1994. "Anxious about jobs" pp.14-15.

9.   Daly, H. and Cobb, J., 1990.*For the Common Good - redirecting the economy towards community, the environment, and a sustainable future.* London, Green Print.

10.   Jackson, T. and Marks, N., 1994.*Measuring Sustainable Economic Welfare - A Pilot Index: 1950-1990.* Stockholm, Stockholm Environment Institute.

11.   Templet, P.H., Glenn, J. and Farber, S., 1991. Louisiana ties environmental performance to tax rates,*Environment Finance.* Autumn, pp.271-277.

12.   Organisation for Economic Co-operation and Development, 1987. *The Promotion and Diffusion of Cleaner Technology in Industry.* Paris, OECD.

13.   Hooper, P. and Jenkins, T., 1994.*On-line, Off Target: An Evaluation of Cleaner Technology Databases.* Friends of the Earth, London.

14.   Secrett, C. 1993. 'Sustainable futures and Friends of the Earth'. John Preedy

Memorial Lecture, Friends of the Earth Annual Conference, Leicester, 10 September.

15. Jacobs, M., 1991. *The Green Economy: Environment, Sustainable Development and the Politics of the Future.* London, Pluto Press.

16. *Daily Telegraph,* January 1994. "NatWest sheds 4,200 workers".

17. See, for example, Martin, R., 1992. The Economy: has Britain been transformed? Critical reflections on the policies of the Thatcher Era, in Cloke, T.(ed), *Policy and Change in Thatcher's Britain.* London, Pergamon.

18. Wainwright, H. and Elliott, D., 1982.*The Lucas Plan: A New Trade Unionism in the Making?* London, Allison and Busby.

19. *Official Journal.* 94/C180/06. 1st July 1994.

20. Friends of the Earth Netherlands has initiated a research programme in conjunction with groups in southern countries to assess the likely impacts on employment and development in the South of stricter environmental policies in the North.

21. United States Congress Office of Technology Assessment, 1993. *Industry, Technology and the Environment: Competitive Challenges and Business Opportunities.* Washington DC, Office of Technology Assessment

22. Jacobs, M. 1994. *Green Jobs? The employment implications of environmental policy.* A forthcoming discussion paper for WWF UK.

23. Commission of the European Communities, 1992. *Towards Sustainability - A European Community Programme of Policy and Action in relation to the Environment and Sustainable Development.* Brussels, CEC. Volume II.

24. Article 2 as amended by the Maastricht Treaty, includes the objectives of *"harmonious and balanced development of economic activities, sustainable and non-inflationary growth respecting the environment, a high degree of economic performance, a high level of employment and social protection, the raising of the standard of living and quality of life, and economic and social cohesion".*

25. Labour Party Policy Commission on the Environment, 1994. *In Trust for Tomorrow.* London, The Labour Party.

26. Barker, T. and Lewney, R., 1990. Macroeconomic Modelling of Environmental Policies: the Carbon Tax, the Polluter Pays Principle and Regulation of Water Quality, in Barker, T (ed) *A Green Scenario for the UK Economy.* Cambridge, Cambridge Econometrics.

27. International Chamber of Commerce, 1991. *ICC Business Charter for Sustainable Development - Principles of Environmental Management.* Paris, ICC.

28.   World Industry Council on the Environment, 1994. *Environmental Reporting - A Manager's Guide.* Paris, WICE.

29.   Schmidheiny, S. 1992. *Changing Course: a global business perspective on development and the environment.* Cambridge, Mass., MIT Press.

30.   ECOTEC Research and Consulting Ltd, 1993. *Sustainability, Employment and Growth: The Employment Impact of Environmental Policies.* Birmingham, ECOTEC.

31.   International Labour Office, 1989. *Employment and training implications of environmental policies in Europe.* Geneva, ILO.

32.   Fothergill, S. and Guy, N., 1990. *Retreat from the regions: corporate change and the closure of factories.* London, Jessica Kingsley.

33.   Sprenger, R-U., 1984. Pollution control programmes and employment. *IFO Digest.*

34.   *ENDS Report,* No 209, June 1992. "Environmental problems signal closure for coke works", pp.7-8.

35.   *ENDS Report,* No 228, January 1994. "One-third of metal businesses 'badly hit' by pollution controls", pp.6-7.

36.   Hilary Benn, Research Officer for MSF, quoted in *Labour Research,* July 1993, p.10.

37.   Willson, J.S. and Greeno, J.L., 1993. Business and the Environment: The Shape of Things to Come. *Prism,* Third Quarter 1993, pp.5-18.

38.   Organisation for Economic Co-operation and Development, 1985. *Environmental Policy and Technical Change.* Paris, OECD.

39.   Ashford, N.A. and Heaton, G.R., 1979. The effects of health and environment regulation on technological change in the chemical industry: theory and evidence, in Hill, C.T.(ed) *Government Regulation and Chemical Innovation.* American Chemical Society Symposium Series No.109, Washington DC, American Chemical Society.

40.   Allen, T.J., Utterback, J.M., Sirbu, M.A., Ashford, N.A., and Hollomon, J.H., 1978. Government influence on the process of innovation in Europe and Japan, *Research Policy,* 7.2.

41.   Irwin, A. and Hooper, P., 1992. Clean Technology, Successful Innovation and The Greening of Industry: A Case-Study Analysis. *Business Strategy and the Environment,* Vol 1.2, pp.1-11.

42.   *ENDS Report,* No 233. "Waste minimisation project succeeds on Merseyside", p.6.

43. *ENDS Report,* No 209. "Express Foods: Milking cost savings from waste reduction", pp.16-18.

44. Huisingh, D., 1988. *Good Environmental Practice - Good Business Practices.* Berlin, Wissenschaftszentrum Berlin fur Sozialforschung.

45. Hooper, P., 1993. *Public and Industrial Policy for Clean Technology: A Case Study Analysis.* Unpublished PhD thesis, University of Manchester.

46. *The Economist,* October 2nd 1993. "The Green Empire", pp.48-50.

47. Bragg, S., Knapp, P. and McLean, R., 1993. *Improving Environmental Performance: A Guide to a Proven and Effective Approach.* Cheltenham, Stanley Thornes.

48. Biffa Waste Services, 1994. *Waste: a game of snakes and ladders: a benchmarking report on waste and business strategy.* Biffa Waste Services, High Wycombe.

49. Pearce, D. and Brisson, I. 1993. *BATNEEC: the economics of technology based standards.* Oxford Review of Economic Policy. Vol 9(4) pp.24-40.

50. For example, Hoechst even took legal action in the Philippines to prevent severe restrictions being imposed on endosulphan, the active ingredient in one of the firm's best selling products, whose use is already severely restricted in Denmark and Sweden (*Pesticide News* 16. June 1992, p.3. 'Hoechst blocks Philippine government attempts to ban endosulphan').

51. Leonard, H.J. 1988. *Pollution and the struggle for world product.* Cambridge, University Press.

52. International Confederation of Free Trade Unions, *Press release,* 29 November 1993. "Trade unions and environment: the memory of Bhopal".

53. House of Lords, Select Committee on the European Communities, 1993. Session 1992-3, 18th Report. *Industry and the Environment.* London, HMSO.

54. Organisation for Economic Co-operation and Development, 1992. *The OECD Environment Industry: Situation, Prospects and Government Policies.* Paris, OECD.

55. Renner, M., 1991. *Jobs in a Sustainable Economy.* Washington DC, Worldwatch Institute.

56. Assumes a 1:1.5 exchange rate for sterling to ECU.

57. *The Economist,* November 20th 1993. "The money in Europe's muck", pp.109-110.

58. International Finance Corporation, 1992. *Investing in the Environment.* Washington DC, IFC.

59. *Environment and Business,* 22 April 1992, p.5.

60. Joint Environmental Markets Unit and ECOTEC Research and Consulting Ltd, 1994. *The UK Environmental Industry: succeeding in the changing global market place.* London, HMSO.

61. Boehmer-Christiansen, S, SPRU, University of Sussex, *Personal communication,* 2 August, 1994.

62. Skea, J. SPRU. In Open University, Science Matters. 1994. *Acid politics.*

63. Environmental Policy Consultants, 1994. Report on the British Environmental Technology Industry Survey. Presented at the *Environmental Technology '94 Conference,* Birmingham.

64. William Averdieck of Pollution Control and Measurement Europe quoted in *Financial Times,* March 24th 1994. "Legislation drives the innovators".

65. Heaton, G., Repetto, R. and Sobin, R., 1991. *Transforming Technology: An Agenda for Environmentally Sustainable Growth in the 21st Century.* Washington DC, World Resources Institute.

66. Codel International, personal communication, July 22nd 1994.

67. PCME (Europe), personal communication, July 22nd 1994.

68. Southern Science, personal communication, July 22nd 1994.

69. The new Environmental Technology Best Practice Programme is the government's fourth cleaner technology scheme in six years, the last three having been scrapped.

70. MacKenzie, J.J. and Walsh, M.P., 1990. *Driving Forces: Motor Vehicle Trends and their Implications for Global Warming, Energy Strategies and Transportation Planning.* Washington DC, World Resources Institute.

71. Department of the Environment, 1994. *Digest of Environmental Protection and Water Statistics No 16.* London, HMSO.

72. Parliamentary Office of Science and Technology, 1994. *Breathing in our Cities - urban air pollution and respiratory health.* London, POST.

73. Holman, C., 1991. *Air pollution and health.* London, Friends of the Earth.

74. *ENDS Report* 230, March 1994. Dispute over health risks from diesel emissions. pp.6-7.

75. Friends of the Earth, 1994. *Roads to Ruin.* London, FoE. This figure will increase once the exact routes of many road proposals are finalised. In addition, the demand for

aggregate for road building is a major factor in the threats posed to SSSIs by quarrying. 105 SSSIs are threatened by mineral extraction under Interim Development Orders (McLaren, D. and Rice, T. 1993.*The planning time bomb unearthed: threats to sites of special scientific interest from interim development orders.*London, Friends of the Earth.

76. Cox, J. R., 1994. *Head-on Collision 1994: Threats to Important Wildlife Sites and Protected Landscapes from Road Development in South East England.* Lincoln, The Wildlife Trusts

77. Pemberton, M., 1991. *Europe's Motor Industry After 1992: A Review of Single Market Legislation and its Implication.* Report 2090, Economist Intelligence Unit, London.

78. Levett, R., 1994, speaking at the Local Economic Policy Unit seminar. *Jobs and the Environment,* 11th January.

79. *Financial Times,*June 14th 1994. "Toyota plant fails to boost Midlands economy", p.16.

80. European Commission, 1993. *White Paper "Growth, Competitiveness, Employment: The Challenges and Ways Forward into the 21st Century".*EC, Brussels.

81. Schiesser H.K. and Bowers, C. 1992. 'Money, Motors and Myths'. pp.8-10 in *Going Green* 12 November 1992. Environmental Transport Association.

82. Department of Transport, 1993. *The Government expenditure plans for transport 1993-94 to 1995-96.* London, HMSO.

83. This estimate assumes an exchange rate between sterling and the DM of 2.4 and that the costs for both road building and railway construction are similar in the UK and Germany.

84. Simon, D., 1986. Spanning Muddy Waters: The Humber Bridge and Regional Development. *Regional Studies,* Vol 21.1, pp.25-36.

85. Centre for Economics and Business Research Ltd, 1994. *Roads and Jobs - The Economic Impact of Different Levels of Expenditure on the Roads Programme.* Report for the British Roads Federation.

86. Friends of the Earth, *Press Release* June 23rd 1994, "British Roads Federation Jobs Report is Crude and Fundamentally Flawed".

87. *Local Transport Today,*July 7th 1994. "Do roads really bring prosperity? A new report reopens the debate", pp.12-13.

88. Lester, N., 1985. *Strategic Road Enlargement and Industrial Regeneration in London.* London, Greater London Council.

89. Institute of Logistics and Distribution Management, 1992. *Survey of Distribution Costs 1991/2*. Corby, ILDM.

90. European Conference of Ministers of Transport, 1991. *Transport and the spatial distribution of activities - Roundtable 85*. Paris, OECD.

91. Saunders, L., 1976. *Freight transport in the Brewing Industry*. London, Greater London Council.

92. McKinnon, A.C., 1983. The development of warehousing in England. *Geoforum*, Vol 14, pp.389-99.

93. House of Commons Select Committee on Employment, 1988. *Employment Effects of Urban Development Corporations*. London, HMSO

94. *Independent*, April 4th, 1990. "Developers cut back in face of offices glut".

95. Organisation for Economic Co-operation and Development, 1978, Results of a Questionnaire Survey on Pedestrian Zones. Cited in Transport and Environmental Studies, 1989. *Quality Streets*. London, TEST.

96. Confederation of British Industry, 1989. *Trade Routes to the Future*. London, CBI.

97. Cullison, A.E., 1992. Congested Roads in Japan Thwart Just-In-Time Efficiency. *Journal of Commerce*, March 16th.

98. Lowe, M.D., 1994. *Back on Track: The Global Rail Revival*. Washington DC, Worldwatch Institute.

99. International Energy Agency and Barker, 1992. Cited by Barker, T., 1993. Is Green growth possible? *New Economy*, pp.20-25.

100. Taylor, L. 1992. Employment aspects of energy efficiency. In Christie, I. and Ritchie, N. (eds) *Energy efficiency: the policy agenda for the 1990s*. London: Policy Studies Institute.

101. Environmental Resources Limited, 1983. *Jobs and Energy Conservation*. London, Association for the Conservation of Energy.

102. The other studies in Table 2 are based on different scenarios: the ERR report adds a 30 year Combined Heat and Power (CHP) programme to the base of the ACE/ ERL study. The Louisiana figures are derived from an input-output analysis of an energy efficiency investment in the state of Louisiana. The study by Boardman assessed a potential national energy efficiency programme in the UK for the domestic sector only.

103. Krier, B. and Goodman, I., 1992. *Energy Efficiency: Opportunities for*

Employment, prepared for Greenpeace UK by the Goodman Institute, cited in Greenpeace UK's Memorandum of evidence to the House of Commons Employment Select Committee.

104. One TeraWatt hour (TWh) equals 1,000,000 MegaWatt hours.

105. Friends of the Earth, 1993. *Energy Efficiency.*Memorandum of Evidence to the House of Commons Environment Select Committee.

106. Department of Energy, 1994. *Energy Digest 1994.*London, HMSO. The capacity figure is for electricity generation only.

107. Combined Heat and Power Association, research cited in 101.

108. This assumes that the original estimate did not include manufacturing jobs, that CHP provides a total of 0.0042 TWh/year per MW, and that all the displaced capacity, including that for heat generation, provided jobs at the same rate as conventional coal-fired generation.

109. Flavin, C. and Lenssen, N., 1990.*Beyond the Petroleum Age: Designing a Solar Economy*. Washington DC, Worldwatch Institute.

110. Levine, M. D. et al, 1991.*Energy Efficiency, Developing Nations and Eastern Europe - A Report to the US Working Group on Global Energy Efficiency.*Washington, International Institute for Energy Conservation.

111. Friends of the Earth, 1992.*Who Pays the Piper: The Operations of Multilateral Development Banks in Central and Eastern Europe*. London, FoE.

112. For example EBRD has changed its Energy Operation Policy Document to place more emphasis on demand side management.

113. Gipe, P. 1994. 'Overview of worldwide wind generation'. In *Renewable Energy: Climate change, energy and the environment.*Proceedings of the World Renewable Energy Congress. Pergamon Press.

114. BTM Consult, personal communication 22nd September 1994. BTM suggest that the turbines now being installed require less maintenance time (in the range of 230-300 jobs/TWh).

115. Calculated from BTM's estimates of 4.4 jobs per MW installed, and that each MW installed provides 0.0015-0.002 TWh/year.

116. Department of Trade and Industry, 1994. *New and Renewable Energy: future prospects in the UK*. Energy paper 62. London, HMSO.

117. At 4.4 direct jobs and an additional 7.6-11.6 indirect jobs per MW installed,

based on BTM estimates.

118. The figure assumes that no limitation is imposed by integration into the grid.

119. British Wind Energy Association, personal communication, July 22, 1994.

120. *Sustainable Energy News,* March 1994. "Energy and Jobs - against under-development in Latin America", p.3.

121. *ENDS Report,* No 231. "Eco-design initiatives gather momentum", p.29.

122. Cooper, T., 1994. *Beyond Recycling - the longer life option.* London, New Economics Foundation.

123. Friends of the Earth, 1993. *Overpackaging - wasting money, wasting resources.* London, Friends of the Earth.

124. Friends of the Earth, 1992. *Bring Back the Bring Back: The environmental benefits of reusable packaging.* London, Friends of the Earth.

125. ECOTEC Research and Consulting Ltd, 1985. *The Employment Implications of Glass Re-use and Recycling, prepared for the Directorate General for Science.* Research and Development of the Commission of the European Communities.

126. Day, P., Gateway Supermarkets Ltd. 'A retailer's view of packaging re-use'. Paper to PIRA International conference: *Packaging Re-use,* 5th Nov. 1991.

127. Stahel, W.R. and Jackson, T. 1993. Optimal Utilisation and Durability. pp 261-294 in Jackson, T. (ed) *Clean Production Strategies.* London, Lewis Publishers.

128. BBSRC/EPSRC Clean Technology Unit, cited in the ESRC's Global Environmental Change Programme (Phase IV) Research Specification, 1994.

129. Paper Federation of Great Britain, 1994. Industry Facts. London, PFGB.

130. Confederation of European Paper Industries, 1992. *Key Statistics* 1992. Brussels, CEPI.

131. 'Apparent recovery' according to 130.

132. British Waste Paper Association and the Independent Waste Paper Processors Association, personal communication, 1994.

133. Environmental Resources Limited, 1984. *Employment Potential of Waste Recovery and Recycling Activities and Socio-Economic Relevance of Waste Management Sector in the Community.* Report prepared for Directorate General for Environment, Consumer Protection and Nuclear Safety of the Commission for European Communities.

134. James Marsh, DTI, personal communication 14 August 1994.

135. Tellus Institute and Wehran Engineering. Analysis of Solid Waste System Costs for the State of Vermont. Report for Vermont InterRegional Solid Waste Management Committee, cited in 55.

136. Calculated from Department of the Environment. 1991.*Waste Management Paper 28. Recycling - a memorandum providing guidance to local authorities on recycling.* London, HMSO.

137. *Environment Business,* 3rd July 1991. 'Scottish Recycling Study'.

138. Geoff Wright, Environmental Consultant, personal communication, 1994.

139. Joint Memorandum by the Department of Trade and Industry and the Department of the Environment to the House of Commons Select Committee on the Environment, 1993.

140. Hemphill, T.A., 1990. Loans and Grants For Recycling Businesses. *Biocycle,* May 1990, pp.54-56.

141. Pretty, J. N. and Howes, R., 1994. *Sustainable Agriculture in Britain: Recent Achievements and New Policy Challenges.* London, International Institute for Environment and Development.

142. Cited in 141.

143. Committee on the Role of Alternative Farming Methods in Modern Production Agriculture of the National Research Council, 1989.*Alternative Agriculture.* Washington DC, National Academy Press.

144. Nature Conservancy Council, 1984. *Nature Conservation in Great Britain.* Peterborough, NCC.

145. See for example, Lees A. and McVeigh, K. 1988.*An investigation of pesticide pollution in drinking water in England and Wales.*London, Friends of the Earth.

146. Conway, G. and Pretty, J. 1992. *Unwelcome Harvest: Agriculture and Pollution.* London, Earthscan.

147. *Farmers Weekly,* 5 February 1993. "Wild cat treatment really hits the spot". p.54.

148. Bateman, D., and Midmore, P., 1993. *Modelling the Impacts of Policy Change in the Less Favoured Areas.* Aberystwyth Rural Economy Research Paper No93-01, University of Wales.

149. Lampkin, N.H. and Padel, S. (eds) 1994 forthcoming.*The Economics of Organic Farming: An International Perspective.*CAB International. The figures include both family and hired labour.

150. Padel, S and Zerger, U. 'Economics of Organic Farming in Germany'. In 149.

151. Dubgaard, A. 'Economics of Organic Farming in Denmark'. In 149.

152. Uses the current average workforce - 0.035 per hectare (based on MAFF, 1993. *Agriculture in the United Kingdom: 1992.*London, HMSO) and a figure for current organic area of 26,000 hectares.

153. John Dolby, BOAG, personal communication 4-10-94.

154. Ansell, D.J. and Tranter, R.B., 1992. *Set-aside: in Theory and in Practice.*Centre for Agricultural Strategy, University of Reading.

155. Based on Ministry of Agriculture Fisheries and Food. *Press release,* May 6th 1994, "1993 Arable Area Payments Applications County Figures".

156. Peter Midmore, personal communication, 18 August 1994.

157. Friends of the Earth, 1992. Memorandum of evidence. In House of Commons, Environment Committee 1993.*Forestry and the Environment.* Vol. II. London, HMSO.

158. Greig-Smith, P.W. 1990. The Boxworth project. *Pesticide Outlook*Vol 1.3 pp.16-19.

159. UNCED, 1992.*Agenda 21,* para 8.3.

160. For example see HMG, 1994.*Sustainable Development the UK strategy.* London, HMSO, para 3.3.

161. *Environment Watch: Western Watch,* December 3, 1993. "Internal Criticism Delays Plans to Revise EC Impact Assessment Legislation", pp.7-8.

162. Nicole Solomons, AEEU, quoted in*Labour Research,* July 1993, p.10.

163. *ENDS Report,* No 230. "Cleaner combustion technology - a revolution waiting to happen", pp.18-21.

164. *The Economist,* March 12th 1994. "Car Crazy", pp.25-26.

165. Jackson, T., 1992. *Efficiency Without Tears.*London, Friends of the Earth

166. Friends of the Earth, 1993.*Using Financial Instruments and Other Measures to Reduce Waste and Encourage Reuse and Recycling.*Background paper submitted to Department of the Environment.

167. Baumol, W and Oates, W. 1988. *The theory of environmental policy.*Cambridge: University Press.

168. Proops, J., Faber, M. and Wagenhals, G., 1993. *Reducing Carbon Dioxide Emissions: a Comparative Input-Output Study for Germany and the UK*. Berlin, Springer-Verlag.

169. Barker, T. 1994. *Taxing Pollution Instead of Employment: Greenhouse gas abatement through fiscal policy in the UK*. Cambridge, Department of Applied Economics, Energy-Environment-Economy Modelling Discussion Paper No. 9.

170. Sondheimer, J., 1991. Macroeconomic Effects of a Carbon Tax, in Barker, T. Ed., *Green Futures for Economic Growth*. Cambridge, Cambridge Econometrics, pp.39-47.

171. Barker, T.S., Baylis, S. and Madsen, P., 1993. A UK Carbon/Energy Tax. *Energy Policy*, Vol 21.3.

172. Majocchi, A. 1994. The employment effects of eco-taxes: a review of empirical models and results. Paper presented at the *OECD Workshop on Implementation of Environmental Taxes*, Paris, February 1994.

173. Bureau du Plan - Erasme 1993, cited in 172.

174. Deutsches Institut fur Wirtschaftforschung, 1994. *The economic effects of ecological tax reform*. Berlin, DIW.

175. Repetto, R., Dower, R., Jenkins, R. and Geoghegan, J., 1992. *Green Fees: How a Tax Shift can Work for the Environment and the Economy*. Washington DC, World Resources Institute.

176. Pereira, A.F., 1991. *Technology Policy for Environmental Sustainability and for Employment and Income Generation: conceptual and methodological issues*. Working paper of the Technology and Employment Programme, Geneva, ILO.

177. Piachaud, D., 1994. A Price Worth Paying? The cost of mass unemployment. *Economic Report* Vol. 8.6. London, Employment Policy Institute.

178. Royal Commission on Environmental Pollution, 1985, *Managing Waste: The Duty of Care*. London, HMSO.

179. Cited by Hackett, P., 1993. *Trade Unions and the Environment*. London, Trade Unions Congress.

180. Mishan, E. J., 1993. *Economists Versus The Greens: An Exposition and a Critique*. Political Quarterly, Vol. 64.2, pp.22-242.

181. Any addition of the job-gains shown in Table 9 must be treated with care as the assumptions of the different studies may not be compatible, and policy in one area may constrain options in others.

182. The results of econometric modelling cannot be simply added together, and this is therefore probably a very conservative estimate of the additional jobs created if investments in water quality, energy efficiency and renewable energy were pursued alongside policies to enforce the polluter pays principle.

183. This is a typical figure according to econometric modelling - see 169.

Support the work
of Friends of the Earth

Please support the vital research and educational work carried out by Friends of the Earth Trust Ltd.

YES, I'D LIKE TO MAKE A DONATION

1. £100 ☐ £50 ☐ £35 ☐ £20 ☐ £15 ☐
£10 ☐ Other: £ _____

I enclose total of £ _____ cheque/PO payable to *Friends of the Earth* or please debit my Visa/Access/MasterCard:

_____ / _____ / _____ / _____ Expiry date _____ / _____

Signature _____ Date ____ / ____ / ____

My name (Mr/Mrs/Miss/Ms) _____

My address _____

_____ Postcode _____

FURTHER INFORMATION

2. If you would like to receive information about any of the following, please tick as appropriate and enclose a self-addressed envelope:

☐ Friends of the Earth membership
☐ Friends of the Earth publications catalogue
☐ How I can join a Local Group
☐ School Friends: schools membership scheme
☐ Legacies
☐ Covenants

PB 94114501

Please cut out or photocopy this form and send it to:
Friends of the Earth, FREEPOST,
56-58 Alma Street, Luton, Beds LU1 2YZ.
No stamp needed, but your stamp will help save us money.

PHONE 0582 485805 TO DONATE ANYTIME